thirst

thirst

7/07
Christine,
Thanks for
the support!

Linda A Lavid

Best
always!

Linda

Aventine Press

Published by Aventine Press
1023 4th Ave #204
San Diego CA, 92101
www.aventinepress.com

ISBN: 1-59330-407-2

Printed in the United States of America

Passion in all its forms
is a mental thirst,
a fever,
a torturing unrest . . .
James Allen

~ C o n t e n t s ~

~ T h e C a b i n ~

"There are drivers and there are passengers," my father says, "and there are the wannabes." He takes his eyes from the road and glances at me. "Those are the people you got to watch out for."

He hasn't bothered to shave. A patchy gray stubble pokes out along his sagging jawline. Or is he growing a beard?

"A passenger wanting to be a driver," he says, "a driver wanting to be a passenger. Doesn't work."

"Hmm," I manage and focus on the passing scenery. Without snow, late fall in western New York is depressing, as if the dim, colorless landscape were lit by a bare hanging lightbulb. A stark forest of leafless trees encroaches upon the highway. The ground cover is littered with decaying leaves and fallen branches. There are no signs of life, redemption.

1

He continues. "Just as well your mother didn't want to come. Drives me crazy, so tensed up, telling me to slow down, watch out for this, watch out for that. I tell her, 'you drive', but no, she just wants to make me miserable."

I keep quiet. Defending one was used for ammunition later, something like – You know Marge, Christie agreed that you complain too much, especially when I'm driving. Instead I say, "None of this is remotely familiar."

"It's the highway. Built twenty years ago. It'll cut the travel time by half."

"You've gone back?"

"A couple of times."

"How'd the place look?"

"Gone through some changes."

"Good or bad?"

He shrugs. "Hard to say."

I could ask what he means, but I already suspect – storms rage, moss gathers – end of story.

My father pushes a lever and the window hums down. A rush of frigid air breaks into the comfy heat, rattling my eardrums.

He takes a deep breath. "Smell that."

Diffusing into the car is a dank odor reminiscent of wet dirt and worms. I button the collar of my coat.

"Cold?" he asks.

"I'm fine."

"No, no, I want you to be comfortable and enjoy the ride."

thirst

The window then slides up, cocooning us in quiet.

We are heading to the cabin. The one my father owned for three years. He had bought it when my brothers were teenagers and I was around twelve, starting my period, trying to figure out how to curl my hair, wear eye shadow. The drive was an hour and a half over asphalt, then gravel, then dirt. The place had been purchased to reel us in, to keep us from growing up, moving on, but by the time we were teenagers, it was too late. We all wanted to stay in the city. We had lives, lives that were put on hold in the 'boonies', 'the dueling banjo backlands', my brothers would say. Every minute there had been endless. I wonder now if we had electricity.

My father laughs. "Electricity? Of course. And running water and a propane tank. All the comforts."

"But time went on forever," I say, "as if we were in a blackout."

"Problem was you guys didn't like not having a television."

"That must have been the problem – no television."

"But there was plenty to do. We had a radio, books. Your mother brought games, cards."

A memory comes to mind – how after a couple of hours the playing cards stuck together and couldn't be shuffled. "Oh, yeah. Blackjack." And we fall silent.

I was supposed to be taking my mother Christmas shopping, going to the mall, having lunch, but Thanksgiving dinner took a nasty turn when my brothers, Rob and Dan, related anecdotal stories about the cabin, stories that made my mother laugh and my father head for the bourbon. By the time the pumpkin pie was sliced, my father had gone from blubbering to caustic to blubbering again. 'Ingrates' became 'assholes', before he started to weep. It was then, as my brothers corralled their wives and kids and slunk into the night, that I promised to join him on this trip, a hopefully brief detour down memory lane.

Mentally, I begin a Christmas list. My nephews are getting to be a funny age, too old for toys, too young for clothes. I couldn't go wrong with video games, but I don't have a clue.

"So, Dad, what would you like for Christmas?"

He snorts and checks the rearview mirror. "Don't get me anything, honey. Just want you to be happy."

Oh, brother. My parents never talk about my marital status – single and approaching forty, but there's always a lingering sub text in their questions, "Should we set another plate?" , "Did you do anything special for your birthday?" Of course, I could mention Jeff and finally put to rest any assumptions of theirs that I might be too picky, too shy, or a lesbian. But the relationship, at this juncture, is tentative – he still has a wife.

"Dad, I am happy. Does that mean I can cross you off my list?"

No response. Clearly a sign I'd be heading to the men's department to buy something brown. "What's your shirt size again?"

thirst

The car barrels down the forsaken stretch of highway. "Ask your mother."

Amid the desolation, there arise the occasional new builds, full of angles and skylights, tucked neatly into wooded areas flanked by shiny SUVs and satellite dishes. Who'd live there? I assume a large percentage are energy-squandering isolationists with more than their share of disposable income to burn. In reaction, I consider the cabin. Its modest simplicity almost seems beatific.

"When you went back, did you get to see the inside?"

"No, just parked by the road."

"Sorry you sold it?"

"Had no choice."

Whether that was a yes or a no, I couldn't be sure. My recollection was that the ownership of the cabin came to an abrupt halt after both my brothers, one a senior in high school, the other a junior, skipped school, loaded themselves, eight friends (three of whom were sexually compromising young women) along with a keg of beer into a van and drove to the cabin, where, for twelve hours, a party ensued that would have gone unnoticed, except for a bonfire that spread to some adjacent trees threatening to decimate the area's only redeeming feature – the woods. Subsequent to the event, my father was served with papers, taken to court and fined five thousand dollars, an exorbitant fee at the time. Shortly thereafter, the place went on the market and both brothers got jobs in a nursing home kitchen where they had to wear hairnets. I was thrilled.

"Why not look for a place now?"

He fiddles with the rearview mirror. "Wouldn't be the same."

I have no parry, no words of consolation, support. Perhaps chasing the past, then reeling it forward is trickier than one would suspect.

For the third time that day, I check the signal on my cell. Jeff promised to call. He's probably en route as well, heading back to Chicago from his in-laws in Cincinnati. Holidays for him and his wife are still spent together for the sake of the generations both above and below. There's no reason to do otherwise. My commitment to anything long term is likewise uncertain. At least for now.

From the highway, an exit looms. My father puts on the blinker. "We're almost there." We veer to the right. He's staring ahead. The corners of his mouth are relaxed in a faint smile.

Soon we're maneuvering along a worn country road that curves, rises and falls. Scrubby homes with mismatched windows, peeling paint, hug the road. Rusty Interstate signs and mailboxes that stand on crooked posts roll by. The newfound wealth and mini-estates seen from the thruway have not stretched this far. Signs of life appear. A cat stares out beneath a car without plates; a Shepard-mix, chained to a tree, freezes. The forsaken animal bares his teeth and lunges at us. His eyes bulge as the taut chain yanks hard. The dog yelps in pain, then cowers. God, get me out of here.

Before long, the car slows. Less than twenty yards ahead is a sign with an arrow. I decipher the faint lettering – Sherwood Lane – and my father makes a left. Immediately, we are facing a steep incline. The Chevy engine revs up, sounding heavy, lumbering. Gravel spits out from beneath the tires. I grab the hand rest. The angle is unsettling, unnatural in a car, prone as if in a dentist's chair. How could I have forgotten this? Still, one thing is familiar – my ears pop like before.

The dismal road tightens even more, barely wider than a single drive.

"Are you sure there are still houses up here?"

His judges the sides. A wayward branch scrapes the car. "Of course."

Barely perceptible the path splits and a more reasonable incline appears. He navigates a slow, bumpy turn. Within moments, I'm sitting upright but the progress has slowed. My heart is beating hard and I want this to be over. What if we can't turn around or crash and burn into a ravine? Miraculously, however, there's a clearing. I lean toward the dashboard.

"It's coming," my father whispers.

An open area yawns before us. The road widens and there's order to the otherwise untamed woods. Grass is planted on both sides of the gravel road. To the right, lined-up railroad ties prevent a roll down a disappearing embankment. On the left, grass climbs a sloping mound. My glance travels up the hill. There it hovers, staking a solid claim in the wilderness.

The cabin's mostly hidden behind a sizable, protruding deck. Propped and leveled by huge posts and crossbeams, the porch extends well beyond the sloping hill. Attempts to hide the underpinnings have begun. Sheets of lattice are tacked on in some spots.

He turns off the ignition. "This is it. What do you think?"

"That deck. It's new, right?"

"Yeah, wasn't here last time." He surveys the area. "Gotta be a great view from up there."

"Hmm."

"Maybe I'll just get out for a minute and stretch my legs."

I don't like the sound of this. "You're not going up there, are you? Dad, it's not our property."

"Don't be silly. Can't do any harm to take a look."

I'm horrified. Sure it's an empty building, but there's something creepy about my father nosing around like some stalker. "Dad, they probably have motion detectors or alarms."

"Christie, I'm not going to break in. Come with me."

Not wanting to either stay behind or head up the hill, I begin to protest when a disembodied voice calls out, "Looking for someone?"

The human voice is unnerving. At first I'm not sure where it's coming from. Then, I see.

thirst

Standing on the slope, half-hidden in the shadow at the far side of the deck, is a stocky, gray-haired man in a flannel shirt.

I lean toward my father. "We should leave. Tell him we're lost."

"Don't be silly," Dad says. He pops open the door, gets out and calls up. "We used to live here. I'm with my daughter to see the place."

"Want to take a better look?" The guy waves. "Come on up."

"Sure it's no bother?"

The two men's voices echo, sounding louder than they should.

"Hell, no. Good to have company."

The place must be doomed. Not only off the beaten path, but a portal, once entered, leaves every soul desperate for stimulation.

Dad turns. "C'mon Christie. Let's see the place."

My imagination slams into overdrive. Who is this guy? Where's his car? How many city slickers has he shot and buried?

"Dad, I don't think – "

"Suit yourself," he says and turns on his heels.

My father doesn't climb the grassy slope but walks toward a timberline where a gravel driveway turns upward. I now recall a circuitous route that travels up and around the cabin, which then merges into the road we just came off of. I re-evaluate the man. On second glance, he appears less sinister. He's wearing wire-rimmed glasses and Dockers.

9

thirst

My father climbs the driveway and the man walks down to meet him. They shake hands, then both look appraisingly at the cabin. What the heck, and I get out of the car.

"Bought the place three years ago," the man says as we enter through the side.

The kitchen area is no longer. Gone are the metal cabinets and cracked linoleum floor. I'm standing in a mud room. The walls are knotty pine and the tile floor is ceramic. A blue and white gingham café curtain covers the lone window that, from the upper half, shows the woods behind. Cubbies, like the kind used in Kindergarten classes, line one wall. Some coats and sweaters are hanging inside. Footgear – Rubber Duckies, winter boots, slippers – are neatly paired and resting on a mat.

My father reaches down to untie his shoes.

"Don't bother," the man says. "Wife's not here."

My father nods knowingly and we cross another threshold.

The first uncensored words from my father are, "Holy shit."

I'm likewise awed. We are standing in the back of a large room with a finished, vaulted ceiling dotted by recessed lighting. The room is remarkably bright, glowing, actually. Soft beige walls and an open floor plan fill the expanse. A modern, downsized kitchen with stainless steel built-ins fits snugly into a U-shaped corner. Nailhead leather furniture, a couch and two chairs with ottomans are placed strategically around a gas fireplace. Beautiful Navaho-design rugs cover the floor. But all this is secondary to the view.

10

thirst

At the far side, where the deck has been added, there's a double bank of sliding glass doors. I'm drawn forward.

Standing on the precipice but still inside, I look toward a westerly direction. The sun, lowered in the sky, is breaking through some clouds. We are on very high ground. A sea of pine trees spreads out before me. But it's the sky that's the most breathtaking. Striations of color – purple, pink, green – consume the vista. Never have I seen such majesty. "What a view," I say.

There's no response. I turn around. The man is pulling down a hidden ladder at the far end.

"Has a loft. Threw in a couple of windows. Sleeps four comfortably. Great for the grand-kids."

My father nods but seems distracted. "You've done a lot of work."

"I'll say. The place was too confined. Needed to open it up."

My father steps toward a door, the only room separate from the great room. "Was this the back bedroom?"

The man turns the knob and pushes the door open. "Not anymore. Made it into a full bath. Separate shower. Tub's got some jets."

My father glances inside. "A lot of tile work. Must have cost a pretty penny."

"Son-in-law did it. He's a plumber. Not too expensive. When did you own the place?"

"Long time ago, twenty-five years or so. Just a getaway, you know."

thirst

The word *getaway* makes me smile. I want to say, "get-as-far-away," but I don't. I then think about myself and Jeff. "Do you ever rent it out?"

The man shakes his head. "Nah. It's only empty for a couple of weeks in the spring. We go golfing."

Ironically, I'm disappointed.

"Christie," my father says, "we need to head back. Your mother's probably making dinner."

The man says, "Bring your wife sometime. Door's always open."

"Thanks for the offer but my wife . . . well, she doesn't care for the country."

Back in the car, I say, "What a place."

My father shrugs. His excitement has waned.

"And that view. How could I have forgotten something like that?"

My father revs up the car. "They tore down all the trees in front. Place is nothing more than a glorified suburb."

"What?"

"All fancy, smantcy."

There's no point in arguing. I pull the seatbelt across and click it on. The strap presses on my cell. Before we head back, I make sure it's still working then place it on my lap. By the time we reach the thruway, my eyes are feeling dry and heavy.

At four-thirty we pull up to the house. Not only has the winter darkness seeped into the afternoon hours, but the home blends in too easily with the surrounding shadows. Neither the kitchen nor living room lights are on. The home looks as if the residents are out, perhaps gone on a vacation.

Dad swerves onto the driveway. "Your mother must still be shopping with Aunt Pat."

"Maybe they went to dinner."

But once inside, a light is shining from beneath my parent's bedroom door.

"Mom?"

A weak voice answers. "I'm in here."

Dad throws his keys on the table and heads to the bathroom.

I knock lightly.

"Come in," my mother says.

Still dressed, she's lying on top of the made bed with an afghan draped over her.

"Taking a nap?"

"Yes."

But she's lying. Crumpled tissues are piled on the bed stand. Her eyes are bloodshot.

"How was the trip?" she asks.

"Mom, what's wrong? Are you sick?"

"I have a headache."

"But your eyes are swollen. Have you been crying?"

She puts her finger to her mouth, then nods toward the open doorway. "Where's your father?" she whispers.

"In the bathroom. Why?"

She leans forward. "Close the door."

None of this is unusual behavior. Whenever I'm around, my parents take the opportunity to gossip about each other. I shouldn't appease her, but I do.

After shutting the door, I return to the bed and sit on the edge. "So what's up?"

"What was it like?" she asks.

"What was what like?"

"The cabin."

"Oh. You wouldn't have believed it. The place is gorgeous. Totally redone on the inside."

She rears back, looking horrified. "You went inside?"

"The owner was there. Gave us a tour."

"And how was your father?"

"I'm not sure what you mean."

"How did he react?"

"Didn't seem impressed."

She has a spurt of energy and sits taller. "Really?"

"Yeah. Here's this absolutely great place and he was totally nonplused." I shake my head. "Seemed like he missed the old place."

My mother's face freezes. Suddenly, her eyes well up and she's reaching for another tissue.

"What's wrong?"

"Nothing. I'm just emotional."

"Doesn't seem like nothing – "

There's a knock at the door.

My mother grabs my wrist. "I can't see him like this."

At the door I peek out. "Mom's not feeling well."

He stretches his neck, trying to look inside.

"I think she could use some soup. Would you mind?"

"Right, I'll run down to Chin's and get some wonton."

"Great idea."

Back on the bed, I say. "Okay, what's going on?"

She slams her fist on the mattress. "That damn cabin."

"Mom, what's with you and the cabin?"

She gives me a hard look. "You don't know? Your brothers never told you?"

"Told me what?"

Her voice is remarkably forceful. "About your father's love nest."

"Excuse me?"

Her face crumbles. "Oh, Christie. He used to go there with Mrs. Lambert, the woman who lived next door."

Lambert. Lambert. Yes, she had two young children. A redhead. "Mom, you sure?"

"Your brothers found them. They had skipped school and saw them together with their own eyes. Through the window in the back bedroom."

The floor suddenly seems to slant. The story can't be believed. But then . . .

thirst

"The fire wasn't accidental, Christie. Your brothers were so upset with your father, they tried to burn the place down."

I jump from the bed. "WHAT?"

"Christie, please don't be upset. I just – "

"Everyone knows about this except me?"

She reaches out. "Honey, you're not the only one. Your father doesn't either."

"Mom, that doesn't make sense."

"Oh, Christie, he doesn't know that I know or that the boys know."

"You two never talked about it?"

She looks small and scared. "God no. I couldn't, not ever."

I return to the bed and put my arms around her. "Mom, I'm sorry."

She's trembling. The bones in her back feel brittle. If I squeeze too hard, they might break.

"Everything's fine," I say. "Besides, that was years ago."

Sniffling, she pulls away. "It was his idea to run out for the soup."

I'm confused. "Yes."

"Then he must still care. At least a little bit."

Suddenly my cell rings. I pull it from my pocket and glance at the read out – Jeff. The incessant, intrusive ring is called dancing raindrops.

"Honey, aren't you going to get that?"

thirst

With each cloying tone the pull to answer it weakens. I turn off the power. "It's not important."

~~~~~

Author's Note:

Thematic to fiction, to life, is the secret. Cloaked and stored away, a secret by nature is hidden, but how can something missing cause so much intrigue, fury, damage? And where, when, how does it reveal itself? Think of your own history. Certainly, there are many secrets stored away to deny, revise reality. Maybe you are the keeper of the secret. Maybe you are the one kept in the dark. No matter. Whatever your position you have a story to tell. The Cabin was first published in The Southern Cross Review.

~ O d e t o S e r l i n g ~

Behind the professor, up high and over the powdery green board, is a clock that has the unnerving habit of jerking from one minute dash to another. The student considers that void, the white space between the markers, and listens, cutting out the sounds of shuffling feet and coughs. Riveted to the clock, she counts off seconds – one Mississippi, two Mississippi – anticipating when another segment of time, swallowed up by eternity, will pass. Suddenly, she is struck by her own criminal boredom. What's the point of such wastefulness? She pulls her gaze away and blinks at the philosophy professor, a man thick around the middle with black-frame glasses. His lips are moving. "To understand Kant's Categorical Imperative . . ." And the sentence dissolves into jargon. Her mind segues to other profundities – What he's like in bed? And would his predilections complement her own?

19

thirst

He has the habit of striding across the room, talking to the air in front of him, flailing his arms on occasion. He's in his own world, the world of ethics and righteousness and dead men. He stops, faces the class and makes an emphatic point – "morality must be rational." She scribbles his words into a notebook for short-term future reference. The value of such obscure wisdom only lasts a semester when it can be regurgitated on an exam or paper then duly forgotten. She looks back up.

He adjusts his glasses, an idiosyncratic trait, then continues the path he has microscopically worn in the linoleum. She imagines the bridge of his nose is red and permanently marked from the constant rubbing of plastic against flesh.

"Universality must be applied in Kant's theory of ethics. Do as we do, not do as I do, if you will."

His words are meaningless, so removed from her own reality. Still, his passion for the topic is endearing. Passion in any form, she has decided, is admirable. Without it nothing would be invented or cured; no mountain climbed, no stone left unturned. Still, what drives passion may thwart other sensibilities. His pants have a sheen to them, as if he has worn them too long and regularly. His shoes are especially troubling. They are sneakers of no particular brand, most likely comprised of synthetic material that harbors foot odor caused by happily multiplying bacteria, perhaps spirilla, tailed and energetic. She'd rather not dwell on this. She listens.

thirst

"For your assignment, take any one of the Ten Command-ments, apply Kant's Categorical Imperative and argue a case for validation. Any questions?"

He looks into the well of the class and, for the first time, his glance becomes personal. In the briefest of moments, they connect. Each other's face is somehow taken in by his and her optic nerves, flashed upside down, then inverted until each brain has an image. And, remarkably, with this image neurons cross the great divide and an explosion of sorts begins. Suddenly she feels heated. Pheromones are released and a corner is turned. His nakedness is imagined. Doughy, she suspects, and more jiggly than she's used to. Still, there may be some quirk, some odd trait that she'll be able to focus on, that will feed the pre-orgasmic state, the growing crescendo of heat and point of no return. But what? His smell, perhaps the hint of cologne, something lemony that soon evaporates as their hearts pound away, as their thrusts take on a life of their own.

He scans the class for any hands. None are being raised.

She then wonders – is he an open-eyed lover or does he prefer to keep his eyes closed? Mentally, she removes his glasses. Nothing is more naked than a person without their glasses. His eyebrows are bushy. That much she can tell. But are his eyes beady or a speckled hazel that changes color? Does it matter? She moves on. There's no telltale sign of any sexual organ, no slight bulge or thickness off to the side. Apparently, it's neatly

21

tucked away, buried in layers of material that have been zipped and buttoned. Or maybe it's retracted and minuscule. Her gaze drops to his feet. Yes, maybe so. Still, there's hope. He may be the kind of man, who, realizing his limitations, tries harder, who understands nuance – the whisper, the squeeze, the spot both hidden and not. Intellectuals are like that, full of rampant curiosity and experimentation. There may be potential here.

"Very well," he says. "See you on Friday." And notebooks are slammed shut.

~~~

The professor lives in a rented room where, when he's not translating obscure Hegelian passages, he surfs websites for cheap DVDs that can be delivered in plain brown wrappers. Intermittent among errant pages of his dissertation are *Girls Gone Wild,* Volumes One through *ad infinitum.* Philosophy and sex are the two driving forces in his life and, he would argue, the entwining roots of any great historical movement. Case in point, take any war for instance, or the Age of Enlightenment. Who can deny or refute that the seminal cause of either is the respective enslavement (war) or freedom (invention) of sexuality and thought. And for this reason, he considers himself a total man, a manly man, who approaches life with both vigorous intellect and a staunch appetite for sex, with or without a partner.

The woman in the second row seems interested. He knows the signs – the unblinking stare, the subtle nod for him to continue. To test the waters, he walks to the window. If her eyes are still on him, there may be a budding opportunity to both explain Phenomenology and slap her rear, make her moan.

It is the beauty of his job – friendly banter with colleagues on the meaning of life during the day, sexual excursions in the evening hours with female students who want a story to tell when they return home for the holidays – a story, he is fairly certain, about a smoldering philosopher who rocks their world.

He turns, and yes, the young woman remains intrigued. Her note-taking has suddenly stopped and no matter where he steps, her eyes follow. He assesses.

She is not unattractive, although he prefers blondes, ones with cantaloupe breasts that pull at buttons and have trouble being contained; breasts that stay full and perky no matter what position she's in, breasts that respond to his every tweak and nibble. Unfortunately, however, this woman is seated, and of course, clothed. What lurks beneath the sweatshirt remains a mystery, but then mysteries are meant to be probed, savored, solved, and he is always up for the challenge. That is not to say there isn't a recurrent snag, a complication of ethics, specifically whether her charms can be averaged into her grade as extra credit. In the past, this has been an issue and he's felt rather used. So he plays by two explicit rules that must be mutually agreed upon before any bodily fluids are exchanged – neither party can be disparaging of a person's belief or weight. Everything else, including getting a D for the course, is fair game.

thirst

He doesn't know her name and would prefer not to, never to. There's something about anonymity that excites him, like in the videos. Few words are exchanged, some vulnerability is shown, and magically clothes come off. The move. He's tried many but finds one particularly successful assuming she lingers at the end of class and fumbles with her notebook. How coy some girls can be, and how so very predictable. The chase is such a curious blend of feigned advance and retreat, a dance, a cha cha cha. His motor is running.

~~~

At 10:50 a.m. in Baldy Hall on the university campus a collision is about to take place. Signals are misconstrued. Flashing lights are ignored. It can't be helped. It is the nature of magnetic fields.

"Hello," he says.

"Hi," she responds.

~~~~~

Author's Note:

Across a crowded room, a glance is exchanged. You've experienced it, sworn by it, rued the day of it. Chemistry. Most times, unfortunately, it's a disaster and you'd be better off meeting someone your mother picked out. I had several titles for this story but finally settled on "Ode to Serling." It came to me as I wrote "At 10:50 a.m. in Baldy Hall . . . " and heard in my head his gravelly, deadpan voice. Rod Serling lives on.

~Third Wheel~

"I've overbooked," Lauren said to her roommate. "You've got to help me out."

"Overbooked?"

"Two guys are coming over tonight and I thought I'd hand one over to you."

Janie stopped chewing the gum. "What do you mean, 'hand one over'?"

Lauren turned to the mirror, pursed her lips, and ran her fingers through her long blond hair. "Well, not hand one over, but share. You know, temporarily."

Standing behind her friend, Janie peered into Lauren's reflected image. Two women couldn't be more different. When compared to Lauren's crystalline blue eyes and pouty lips, Janie's frizzy black hair and space between her two front teeth were an abomination. Janie said, "I don't understand."

"I'm not sure who I like better. So I figured I'd have a group date."

"Group date? But – "

"Janie, c'mon be a sport. Besides you haven't gone out in a while."

"Don't rub it in."

"I'm not rubbing it in." Lauren turned to her friend. "You need to get out. You're home every night. It'll be fun."

Janie stuffed her hands into her pockets. Her inclination was to say no, but how? They had been friends since the seventh grade. Lauren had, for reasons unknown, welcomed Janie into her clique when suddenly Janie reaped the benefits of cool by association, something Janie, who was painfully shy, was forever indebted.

"Don't you think they'll get mad?"

"Could happen.   But I don't want anyone who's overly possessive. Besides it's just a test drive."

Janie rolled her eyes. Test drive. She hadn't been on a test drive or date in more than two years, and for a gainfully employed woman with a nice personality in her mid-twenties, that had to be some kind of record. "Are we going to hang out around the apartment? Rent a movie or something?"

"Heck, no. Let's go for sushi."

Janie felt uneasy. Sushi was expensive. Who was going to pay for what? Sitting around the house, where she'd be anyway, was one thing, but going to a restaurant and sticking some guy with a hundred-dollar tab seemed, well . . . manipulative.

"How about going to that Greek place?" Janie suggested.

"No, it's settled. We'll do Japanese. I'm dying for some warm Saki."

Janie wasn't sure what to wear. Not so much for herself, but she didn't want the guy, whichever one he was, to feel embarrassed.

After forty-five minutes, her room was strewn with balled up skirts, sweaters, pants that she had tried on and tossed off. Finally, she settled on a pair of jeans and a white shirt, the only top that had been professionally washed, starched, and ironed. She stood in front of the closet mirror. She looked clean and decidedly uncomplicated, which meant in her own mind – sexless. She shrugged. What did it matter? Janie slapped on some blush, lip-gloss, and flicked off the bedroom light.

Ten minutes later, Lauren swept into the living room in a cloud of Opium. Her black slacks were pencil-thin and the red V-neck sweater clung. Janie's only hope was that one of the guys was myopic.

Lauren held out a silver chain. "Help me with this will you?" She then raised the cascade of golden hair off her neck.

"So who are these guys?" asked Janie.

"One's an absolute dream. Comes into the shop every day. Orders an *espresso* and gives me a two-dollar tip. His name is

Terrence. The other's Mike. I've talked about him. He's the guy who works on my car. Very nice."

Janie hooked the clasp. "But why not see them separately?"

"I'm not getting any younger. In three years I'll be thirty. That's ancient, so I've decided to get serious and step up the process. The more people you get to know, the better the odds. Law of probabilities, y'know?"

"I suppose, but –"

"Oh, there's the buzzer." Lauren stepped back and stood straighter, sucking in her already-flat tummy. "Do I look okay?"

"Beautiful. How about me?"

Lauren made a quick assessment. "Very sweet," and rushed to the door.

A man cloned from Johnny Depp, pale, dark and smoldering, entered.

"Hey Terr," Lauren said.

"What's up, doll?"

Their eyes locked. After a hanging moment, Lauren pulled her gaze away. "Oh," she said, "this is my roommate, Janie."

Trying to hide her teeth, Janie plastered a tight smile on her face. "Hi," she mumbled.

His glance sailed over her, then riveted back to Lauren. "You're lookin' hot. Where we goin'?"

"Kyoto's."

Janie's stomach lurched. When and how was Lauren going to break the news that the date was a communal one?

"Terr, Janie's coming with us."

His face froze. "To the restaurant?"

"Is that a problem?"

Janie's palms broke out in a sweat. If only a trapdoor would open.

His eyes flitted from girl to girl. He stammered, "I guess not . . . We goin' soon?"

"Actually, I invited someone else too."

"Oh?"

"Yeah, Mike Martin."

"Do I know him?"

Lauren smiled brightly. "Don't think so. He's my mechanic. Come, sit down. I'll get you a beer."

Terrence dropped onto the edge of the couch. "Good idea."

Janie trailed behind Lauren. "I'll help."

Her roommate flagged her away. "Don't be silly. You two get acquainted."

Terrence sat back, then brushed some lint off his sports coat.

Janie slumped into a chair. Her mind raced with what to say. She could always open with some inane remark about the weather, maybe the wind chill. But the inside of her throat felt as if she'd swallowed a wad of cotton. She blurted, "I hear you're an *espresso* man."

"Huh?"

"The kind of coffee you drink."

"Yeah," he said.

"One sugar or two?"

"I drink it black."

"Black, no kidding. That's . . . very manly."

He appraised his fingernails. "Did you say something?"

"Yes. I said – " A buzzer sounded. Janie leapt from the chair. "I'll get it."

Man Number Two had red hair and smelled of aftershave.

She opened the door wider. "Hi, I'm Janie, Lauren's roommate."

He walked inside and grinned. "Nice to meet you, I'm Mike." His eyes then fell on Terrence. The two men glared at each other.

With rising panic, Janie said, "Mike, this is Terrence. Have a seat. I'll get you a beer." She then bolted into the kitchen.

Lauren was slicing limes.

"I don't think this is going to work out," Janie whispered.

"Why not?"

"Someone's going to get the short straw."

"Don't be silly."

"Lauren, neither of them looks happy."

"That's ridiculous."

"But each one thinks they're going out with you."

Lauren twisted off the cap on a bottle of beer. "That's okay. I got it covered. I'm going to flirt with both of them."

"What? How can you do that? Everyone's together."

"Piece of cake."

Janie folded her arms and leaned against the counter. She looked at the clock. It was going to be a long evening.

"Don't look so glum. Here, take a swig."

Janie took the beer. Not bothering with the lime, she put the bottle to her lips and drank what she could manage.

When they returned to the living room, the two men were sitting on opposite ends of the couch.

Lauren placed down the tray of drinks and sat between them.

Within five minutes, her infectious laugh had each man smiling, and by the time the foursome left for the restaurant, Lauren's arms were locked between them.

Kyoto's was upscale. Black-lacquered tables and chairs, along with lit pillar candles warmed the atmosphere. Soft-spoken couples huddled together.

Hidden behind the menu, Lauren said, "Let's get some combination plates."

"A little yin, a little yang," Mike said cheerfully. "Sounds good to me."

Terrence rolled his eyes and called the waiter over. "Bring me a double Scotch."

After ordering enough food for a small wedding, Lauren excused herself to the bathroom with Janie in tow.

While adjusting her lipstick, Lauren considered each prospective beau. "Terr is so handsome, but Mike is not without charm. He's easy to talk to and can fix my car. But Terr, well, he's a major hunk. What do you think?"

Janie shrugged. It was a mute point. After all, what did it have to do with her life? Reluctant to make any choice that was clearly not hers, she said, "They both seem nice."

"Yes, that's true. I'll just have to see who's going to try harder."

Janie didn't have a response for that.

When the women returned to the table, Mike was sitting alone.

Lauren slipped into the seat. "Is Terrence in the bathroom?"

"Actually, he just walked out."

Lauren stiffened. "You're kidding, right?"

"Don't think so. He got up, and a minute later, I saw him pass by the front window."

Lauren reached for Terrence's crumpled napkin. "Did he leave any money?" She shook it. "Nothing? What the – "

"Listen, don't worry about it," said Mike. "I'm with two beautiful women. We can still have a great time."

Janie beamed. Never had she been likened to her gorgeous roommate.

Lauren pulled her cell from her purse and punched in some numbers. "He's not getting away with it. He ordered a double Scotch for chrissake!"

Mike shrugged.

Janie tried to think of something to say, something clever, something to cut the tension.

Lauren pulled the phone from her ear and flipped it closed. "He's not answering."

"It's not the end of the world," Janie finally said.

Flushed, Lauren looked around the restaurant. "I'm going to use the pay phone at the bar. That punk won't know it's me calling. Be back in a sec." She sprinted from the table.

Just as Janie suspected the evening was a disaster. Beneath the table she picked at her cuticles, resisting every urge to begin biting her nails.

Mike leaned toward her. "That guy wanted me to leave with him."

"What?"

"I told him, No way."

Confused, Janie asked. "Why was that?"

A smile that lit up the room broke across his face. He reached for her arm. "I just met the girl I'm going to marry."

~~~~~

Author's Note:

I had sent Third Wheel to two publications. The first editor felt Lauren was too despicable and unlikeable for print. The second market kept the story for two years. They loved it, then went out of business. The trials. In any event this was a fun story to write.

thirst

Just desserts are served, and a modern day Cinderella finds a nice guy who can fix cars. Even better than a prince.

~ D M V ~

Nothing was going to ruin Mia's afternoon, not the rain, not the long line she was standing in at the DMV. The wall clock read 12:15. Paul expected dinner at six. Figure two hours for the sauce, add in the shopping, prep, and there was plenty of time. Heck, time to burn. Relax. What a dingbat.

In the line she shifted her weight and considered the menu, his favorite, Chicken Parmesan – fresh chicken, not frozen, vine-grown tomatoes, not hothouse, and of course grated cheese, none of that powdered stuff like last time. Oh, she almost forgot. She dug a pen and slip of paper from her purse. *Grater,* she wrote in a jittery script.

She'd have to make up for the morning. She was just tired. The flight from Cancun had been a bear – stuck in the Atlanta airport with no sleep, no shower, and junk food for twenty-four hours. She woke up with a dull headache and couldn't get into it. She'd make up for everything tonight. Put on a negligee, give him a little show. Maybe the black lace or the thong and push-up. But she'd have to try them on first, take a good look at herself in the three-way and make sure she didn't look fat.

Inside her pocket the cell vibrated. She fished out the phone and flipped it open. "Hello?"

"Hey, baby."

"Hi, honey."

"Been calling the house. Where are you?"

"At the DMV. Remember?"

"Oh yeah. Listen, about this morning. I'm really sorry. Won't happen again."

"It's okay."

"Had a lot on my mind. Getting back to work after the honeymoon, the stress, the craziness. Man, I don't know what I was thinking."

"No problem, really."

"I'm the luckiest man alive. About tonight, forget dinner, let's order out."

"But I want to try the recipe again."

"Baby, cooking isn't your strong point. We'll order Chinese. Besides I've been thinking," his voice became a whisper, "maybe we could get the camera out and make another movie."

"Paul . . ."

"I love you so much."

"I love you too."

"And big daddy loves you too. Do you love big daddy?"

"Oh, Paul, I – "

"Say it."

Mia glanced around, cupped her hand to the phone and murmured, "I love big daddy."

"Atta girl."

"Next," a disembodied voice called out.

Mia glanced around. She was first in line. "Honey, I gotta go."

"Sure baby. See you tonight. Can't wait. Love you."

"Love you too."

Disconnected, she pulled the phone from her ear, snapped it shut and headed for the teller.

"What do you need?" said the woman at the window.

Mia passed the form. "Change of name."

The woman checked it over then turned toward the computer. Her fingers flew over the keyboard. Tat-tat-tat.

Mia's hands shook. She loved Paul totally. Things would be fine.

"Okay," said the woman, swiveling around. "Sign at the X."

Mia picked up the pen and wrote, *Mia Fort – .* Midway, she stopped and blinked hard. "Oh no, I'm signing the wrong name."

"No problem. I'll print another."

Mia felt flushed, embarrassed by such stupidity. Tat-tat-tat.

thirst

Moments later a clean form was in front of her.

Mia was about to sign when the woman reached over and grabbed Mia's hand. "Girl, you sure you want to do this?"

How did the woman know? Mia wanted to defend herself, tell the woman that Paul's a doctor and she deeply loved. Instead, she jerked her hand free. *Mia Brockman*, she signed, officially and forever Paul's wife.

Back in the car, Mia pulled down the rearview mirror. She needed to check her make-up, to adjust, to adapt. She needed to not see the black eye.

~~~~

Author's Note:

DMV is flash fiction. Flash fiction runs under 1000 words and is becoming a popular format, especially for the internet. Not so long ago, the main outlet for short stories was obscure university or literary presses that often had a significant turnaround time and whose audience was limited. The game is changing. Express yourself, put it on the information highway, and show the world what you got. DMV was my first award-winning story. It's creepy and hopefully makes a reader think. DMV was first published by Ascent Aspirations Magazine.

~The Restaurant~

"Harry, were we always this boring?"

"Not sure what you mean."

"Look at us. Here we are again on a Thursday night. But it's not night. Not even close. We're eating dinner at four-thirty. The sun's still up. It's hurting my eyes."

"Should we move?"

"No. I'll just keep my sunglasses on."

"Dee, stop whining. We have the senior discount, add that to the early bird special, and dinner's practically on them. Great deal. What's the problem?"

"Harry, the specials are the same every Thursday. Meatloaf and pork chops. And the chef salad comes in ratty wooden bowls, and all we see are very old people wearing too much polyester."

"You're being cruel. Besides, we are them and they are us."

"My God, how can you say that?"

"Take a good look at me."

"Can't see a damn thing with these sunglasses. Besides I'm wearing jeans, *cotton* jeans."

"You used to like this place."

"The first and second time maybe. But it's been over a year and here we sit. It's become our life, an extension of who we are."

"Where's the waitress? I'll order you a drink."

"That's your answer to everything isn't it, Harry?"

"It's not my answer to everything. However, it is my answer for the moment. Manhattan. Martini. What will it be?"

"Just water."

"Miss, one Martini, very dry, with a side dish of olives."

". . . She's very pretty. Such long legs."

"Yes, I suppose so."

"I was never that pretty."

"You were very pretty."

"That was a long time ago."

"Fishing for compliments?"

"I'm hardly fishing. I'm casting a desperately huge net and taking whatever I can snag."

"In that case you were not pretty at all. You were quite beautiful."

"Coming from you doesn't count."

"Now why is that?"

thirst

"Because you're my husband . . . Don't shake your head. You have to tell me I'm beautiful. Otherwise we'll get into a fight and won't talk for the rest of the meal."

"We may be heading in that direction anyway."

"Okay. Let's start over. I wonder what I'll have tonight? Hmm . . . the meatloaf sounds redundant."

"There are other things on the menu."

"I ordered the steak twice, tough as shoe leather and overdone both times. And we always have chicken at home."

"Try the fish."

"Scrod? What the heck is a *scrod*? Sounds obscene."

"Obscene?"

"Like something that belongs in your pants."

"I think that would be against the health code . . . Good. Here comes the Martini. Sure you don't want a drink?"

"Positive."

"Well, then we're ready to order. The special, one of each. Two salads with the house dressing on the side. Two baked potatoes, sour cream on the side. After that coffee. Thanks."

"Yes, thank you, Miss . . . She must be close to six feet."

"Hmm . . ."

"Do you still look at women, Harry?"

"That's a loaded question."

"I still look at men."

"That's nice."

"Don't you want to know what I look at?"

41

"Their eyes?"

"It's their shoulders and the way they walk."

"Okay, I'll bite. The way they walk?"

"The walk says a lot about a man. Ask any woman."

"How about my walk?"

"You sort of slump."

"Doesn't sound good."

"Not necessarily. Some women might find it attractive. The lost boy thing. But you're my husband and I love you anyway. Besides, I don't think you always slumped. No, I think that came later."

"Changing times, changing ways."

"You never answered my question."

"What was the question?"

"Do you ever look at women?"

"Sometimes they float in my field of vision. Hard not to notice, I suppose."

"What specifically floats in your field of vision?"

"Hmm . . . the way they walk?"

"No fair, you stole my answer."

"I liked your answer. It was a good answer."

"You're cheating."

"I don't think this is a healthy conversation."

"You act like you're afraid of me. What could I possibly do?"

". . . The Martini's nice and dry. The good bartender must be working. Last week the drink tasted like battery acid. But this is smooth. Want a sip?"

"No. So don't answer me. It was a rhetorical question anyway. I know what you look at."

"Really? What then?"

"You like rumps."

"Hmm . . ."

"High ones."

"Yes, you may be right."

"My ass is like a pancake."

"That's not true. It's quite round."

"It's totally deflated."

"You're feeling quite insecure this evening. Is there anything I can do?"

"I just wish the waitress wasn't so damn tall."

"Why do women do that?"

"Do what?"

"Compare themselves."

"Insecurity, I suppose."

"What does her height have to do with you?"

"If my legs were longer, maybe my ankles wouldn't be so thick. Peasant stock, my father used to say."

"I get it now. You wanted approval from your father, an Oedipal thing."

"Electra, actually."

"Huh?"

"Father, daughter is an Electra complex. Oedipal is mother and son."

"Yes, of course. Now I remember, although vaguely."

"And there's the societal pressure to fit the mold. Never too rich, never too thin."

"Where's height in the equation?"

"Stands to reason if you're taller, you're thinner."

"Here come the salads . . . Thank you . . . So, did you learn anything new today?"

"Harry, I despise that question. Why do you always ask me that?"

"Because it's critical."

"How so?"

"Life is about lessons."

"Oh dear, another life quote."

"Humor me. You read the paper, saw the news. Did anything catch your attention? Make you wonder?"

". . . There was one thing. Those floods in the Midwest. How do people get stuck in their houses when they see the water rising? Why do they wait so damn long to leave?"

"They were probably on high ground."

"That doesn't make sense."

"Most likely the water filled the lower areas around them, then, when the waters rose, they got marooned."

"So much for the high ground."

"It has its disadvantage."

"So, Harry, what did you learn today?"

"Thought you'd never ask. Let's see . . . Oh, yes. Apparently Aristotle Onassis put up the front money to get Robert Kennedy assassinated."

"Really?"

"Hmm . . . The two of them despised each other."

"Because of Jackie? Weren't they both in love with her?"

"Possibly, but that was only a small part. I think it was more of an Eliot Ness, Al Capone thing. Good versus evil. All very Shakespearian. Onassis was not a particularly nice guy."

"I suppose you don't get filthy rich by being a nice guy."

"He was a thug."

"And I must say, not very attractive. How did Jackie go from prime rib to . . . what's the word? Oh yes – scrod."

"Money, I suppose."

"Now you see my point."

"And what point would that be?"

"A woman can never be too thin or too rich."

"Oh . . . In that case, I'll eat your croutons if you don't want them."

"About Jackie and John, do you think they loved each other?"

"They were married weren't they?"

"Harry, sometimes you're so concrete. Of course they were married. But that doesn't automatically mean they loved each other."

"I don't agree. They must have loved each other. Why else were they together?"

"For the children. Or maybe for his career, you know to get elected. Or for money, status."

"Guess we'll never know. How about a nice glass of wine?"

"Why did you marry me, Harry?"

"Let me think . . . Oh, yes now I remember. You asked me."

"I most certainly did not."

"You most certainly did. At Crystal Beach."

"Crystal Beach?"

"We were stuck on the Ferris wheel. Sitting on top of the world. You'd had an argument with your parents. Remember?"

"Argument? About what?"

"I don't know. But you said, quite clearly, 'Harry, marry me. Take me away.'"

"I said that?"

"My first and last proposal. Hard to forget."

"If it happened, and I'm not saying it did, it was under duress."

"Duress?"

"Maybe that's when my father had found cigarettes in my coat pocket. Yes, now I remember. He wanted to ground me. Said only trollops smoked."

"Trollops?"

"He was trying to be nice. Then my mother got hysterical and pulled the house apart looking for the rosary."

"And all these years I thought it was about me, about wanting me, being with me. Oh, good here comes the food. I'm hungry."

"I can't get over how tall people have become. I used to be tall. Well, maybe not tall, but average, normal. Now I'm a shrimp and shrinking besides."

"What looks good to you? The meatloaf or pork chops? Or do you want to share?"

"Ugh. I'll try one chop. You have the rest."

"You sure?"

"Positive."

"I don't know why you didn't order something else. Here you go."

"Come to think of it. You never did ask me to marry you."

"Huh? I gave you a ring."

"Yes. But you never got down on one knee. There was never a formal proposal. It was assumed."

"That's ridiculous. Of course I asked you to marry me."

"Really? When? Where?"

"When I gave you the ring."

"The ring. Don't you remember? We picked it out together at the jewelers. On a rainy afternoon. I had just found out I was pregnant with Marnie. We needed to act quickly."

"Oh, yeah."

"Maybe if I hadn't been pregnant, we wouldn't have gotten married."

"That's ridiculous."

"You had said so."

"Said what?"

"That it would have been better to wait, to finish college, buy a house."

"I said that?"

"Yes."

"That must have been your first husband."

"It was after Marnie was born. We were living in that third floor walk-up by the zoo. The couple downstairs banged on the ceiling whenever she cried."

"Oh. All I probably meant was that we should have done things in proper order."

"Proper order?"

"Yes, finish college first, then buy a house, then have children. No matter what, we would have gotten married."

"I wonder . . ."

"I was crazy about you."

"Whatever you say, Harry."

"You're in a very strange mood this evening, have a drink."

"Ever chew linoleum?"

"Huh?"

"The pork chop."

"Send it back."

"When have I ever sent anything back?"

"Suit yourself."

"Harry, did you ever cheat on me?"

"No. Why do you ask?"

"Harry, it wouldn't bother me if you did."

"Well, I never did. I think I'll order another drink. Where's that waitress?"

"I once heard Jayne Meadows say that no matter what Steve Allen did, she'd never divorce him."

"That's nice."

"And you know what Steve Allen said, 'After forty years of marriage, now you tell me?'"

"Cute."

"I always liked Jayne Meadows. Pretty and smart, but not showy, you know?"

"She was on the Honeymooners, right?"

"No, that was Audrey, her sister."

"Right, now I remember."

"Anyway, Harry, I agree with Jayne Meadows. I'd never divorce you, no matter what."

"That's nice."

"So I'll ask you again. Did you ever cheat on me?"

"No."

"Not once? Never?"

"Never, ever."

"Interesting."

"Why is that interesting?"

"What about Luisa?"

"Luisa?"

"Yes, your secretary."

"Don't be absurd."

"1978"

"What about 1978?"

"She came over that Christmas and told me."

"Told you what?"

"That you and she were lovers."

"Nonsense."

"She had proof, Harry."

"I don't want to hear anymore. Oh, there she is. Miss?"

"Notes in your handwriting. Calendar notes signed, *Love, Harry*. Went all the way back to September."

"She was good at signing my name. Had to for all my correspondence. Why are you bringing this up?"

"She said you were playing us against each other, and that we needed to stick together."

"That's ridiculous. Yes, another drink please. And my wife will have a Manhattan."

"Harry, don't order for me. Thank you, Miss, but I don't want anything . . . So whatever happened to Luisa?"

"I can't remember."

"She left. I know that. I have to say I was rather surprised. I called your office and another woman answered, a new secretary. Why did she leave, Harry? "

"Aren't you going to eat your potato?"

"I'm afraid I'm losing my appetite."

"Listen, Luisa was a sweet girl, but nothing ever went on between us. I swear. I'm afraid the girl had an imagination."

"Hmm . . ."

"You don't believe me?"

"Some nights you didn't come home."

"I always came home."

"No you didn't, Harry."

"I should have known if I didn't come home."

"There were no towels, Harry. No tissues in the wastebasket."

"What are you talking about?"

"That year after I spoke with Luisa I took a couple of trips. Remember? Down to Ithaca to visit Marnie in college. You tried to make the house lived in. I'll give you that. But things were missing. No wet towels in the hamper, no tissues in the bathroom wastebasket. Harry, you always nick yourself shaving."

"What do you want me to say? What you want to hear, or the truth?"

"The truth, Harry."

"Well, then here goes . . . I swear I never had sex with that woman."

"Not very original, Harry. And hardly comforting given the circumstances."

"Circumstances?"

"So you didn't have sex with Luisa. It was just you, her and a Cuban Cigar? I don't believe you."

"Dee, let's drop it."

"You're upset."

"I most certainly am not."

"You never knew I knew."

"There was nothing to know."

"I got over it. Eventually. Now I'm just curious. Why did you do it? I thought we were happy."

"We were happy. We still are happy."

"Harry, there comes a point when the truth is important. Life's about lessons, your quote not mine. I'm at that point, trying to learn, figure out things. There's so much about life we'll never know. Then there are those things that we can know if we make the effort. Harry, I – What's that sigh supposed to mean?"

"Nothing."

"What a waste. All these years wondering, wanting to ask. Finally I get the nerve up and – "

"Listen, if it makes you happy. Yes."

"Yes?"

"I had an affair."

"Oh . . . "

"You said you wanted to know."

"I'll have that drink now."

"But you insisted – "

"Make it a double."

~~~~~

thirst

Author's Note:

Dorothy Parker often wrote short stories in dialogue form. I gave it a whirl. Ellipses made the job easier. There's more to the story of Harry and Dee. Their plight continues in the form of a play with the working title of "Scenes From a Marriage (Not Bergman)." From a writing perspective, when I think of marital indiscretions, I also think of diamonds. Both are prism-like, sharpy faceted and uniquely intricate when put under a microscope. This story also begs the question. Does a spouse really want to know?

~ T h e O t h e r W o m a n ~

Shayna sat at the kitchen table, staring into space, where, for the better part of the afternoon, she had been lighting and relighting cigarettes. In the cloud of smoke that settled around her, she closed her eyes, hoping a few minutes of sleep might descend upon her, relieving her of that unrelenting, internal voice – he doesn't love you, he never loved you, he used you, you deserve to be used – but she could neither nap nor stop the refrain, undeserving as she was. She opened her eyes and took another drag. He wasn't the real problem anyway. It was HER, the other woman, the cliché, the whore who wrapped her ankles behind her ears, the bitch who did anything to get him.

Jeremy was defenseless, as many men were, ambushed by feminine guile, undetectable to male radar. Ironic, how men could land on the moon, build towers to the sky, chart the human genome and yet get so easily short-circuited by some horny-assed vamp.

How did it happen? Perhaps, SHE, vigilant to his whereabouts at any given moment, waited for him at the water cooler, and as he approached, SHE, in a skirt as short as her crotch, bent over and filled a cup, allowing him a private, unencumbered view that froze his furtive glance and stiffened him quick, and once the pleasantries started, "Good morning," "Have a good one,", SHE may have seen him in the cafeteria, and as he surveyed the room for an unoccupied table, SHE may have smiled and nodded slightly, as if they shared some history, and perhaps later, SHE followed him to the copier located in a private, closed room and brushed against him, body to body, and his hardness became a hapless, conditioned response, that no man, not even her husband could extinguish, no matter his resolve, no matter the consequences.

When had it begun? Had Shayna missed the clues - a lingering scent, a hang-up call during dinner, a cigarette butt, not her brand, crushed in the truck ashtray? But there were no clues, at least not until three weeks earlier when he moved out. What other proof did she need? After all, a husband didn't go to a motel when he had HBO and crushed ice at home. What would be the point?

Shayna glanced at the clock. Still another three hours until dark and before she could leave. Taking a shower would be a good idea, or opening a can of soup. Instead, she emptied the bullets from the chamber and rolled them in her hot palm. After a few minutes, the cold metal felt liquid. She rubbed the small cylinders along the back of her neck. They rolled across her stiff muscles then slipped from her hand and scattered onto the floor.

In the few short weeks Shayna had been stalking her husband, she had become aware of the ever-changing landscapes, not only of her life, what she believed in, worked for, prided herself in, but in the physical surroundings that had previously gone unnoticed. In a matter of a few weeks daylight had shrunk a full half hour. How insidious darkness could creep into one's life. But it was of great consolation since each minute earlier that the sun set, Shayna could leave her house and finally get down to business.

The motel where Jeremy stayed was located at the entrance to the Interstate, off a six-lane highway in an area of lax zoning ordinances and over development, a shopper's paradise. Car dealers, restaurants, dollar discounts and outlet stores vied for attention, encroaching onto the road with flashing lights and signs a blind man could see, if not with his eyes, with his ears. A constant hum of electricity permeated the area.

Shayna inched the rented beige Taurus beside a dumpster in the McDonald's parking lot, where minutes earlier she had ordered a large black coffee. She rolled her seat back, cracked the window open and took a deep breath, her first of the day. Ironically, in this seemingly desperate situation – alone, outdoors, unprotected – she felt relaxed. Her home, no their home, was like a mausoleum with its echoing silence and chilled, stultified air. But here in the plushy softness of a late-model rental car with everything at hand, she felt safe, cocooned rather than entombed.

The Sweet Dreams Motel was located next door to the McDonald's. From where she parked, Shayna was able to get a clear view of the back half of the motel property, specifically Room 16 on the ground floor.

Initially, Shayna had spied on Jeremy outside his office. Unfortunately, she did not go unnoticed and shortly after her return home, he called her with threats of court action. "Protection from your wife?" Shayna had screeched. "The only one who truly loves you." An abrupt click and dial tone had answered her.

She pulled a cigarette from the pack and stuck it between her teeth. For the past several days during the endless hours of circular thinking, Shayna had revamped her plans several times. Her options vacillated from maiming to murdering, and back again. Killing HER would be a resounding statement but the consequences of murder were distasteful. A life in prison thumbing through innumerable psalms was not her style. No, maiming HER held the ticket, blowing out her knee caps perhaps. Yes, not only would this be painful, but would serve double duty – Jeremy was a leg man. Shayna lit the cigarette and took a drag. Exhaling, she hissed, "Hang up the Manolos, bitch. Dr.Scholl's a knockin'."

thirst

At 7:45 p.m., Jeremy's black bronco heaved up the drive into the parking lot. As it swerved and settled into the slot at Room 16, Shayna perked up. A shaft of light from the room next door illuminated the entire side of the truck. Her heart raced. This could be it. What would Shayna see first? A long tapered leg ending with a stiletto heel?

The seconds seemed interminable as her burning stare rested on the front passenger door. Desperate not to blink, not to miss the moment when the door opened, she kept her itching, watery eyes open through the dense cloud of smoke that hung around her. Haphazardly, she blindly stuffed the lit cigarette into the tray and moved her head closer to the windshield. A slam echoed in the night air. In response and barely perceptible, the truck quaked. Was Jeremy coming around to open the door and give HER his hand? Shayna braced herself by the injustice, the insult, the injury. Reaching to the passenger seat, she grabbed the snubbie.

Seconds passed. Hyper vigilant for any sound, she squinted and turned her head slightly. While the truck blocked the view of her husband, it didn't obstruct the jingling of keys. Damn! He had exited and appeared to be alone . . . or was he? Maybe SHE was already inside, wearing some slutty strings of purple polyester that left nothing to the imagination and stunk to high heaven. After hearing the clap of a shutting door, Shayna weighed her options.

thirst

On previous evenings, Shayna had stayed until the pale flickering television light went out, sometimes as early as eleven, other times as late as two. But how many more hours, days, weeks was she supposed to stand by, remain on hold? She was his wife for chrissake. She had rights by law and in the eyes of God.

Decisively, she made her move and burst from the car. Raising her straight skirt, she climbed over a thick metal guardrail, then stepped down the small incline. Her spiked heels sank into the wet ground. Once on concrete, she walked on the balls of her feet, reducing the familiar clack of her stride. Puffs of condensed air emptied from her mouth as she approached the motel door and its blue numerals. Then, covering the peephole with her finger, she knocked.

"Who is it?" came his muffled voice.

"Your wife."

Long seconds passed before he cracked open the door. His tie was off, his shirt unbuttoned, untucked. "What are you doing here?"

"We need to talk. Or is this not a good time?" she said, peering beyond him into the dim room.

"Are you going to be rational?" he said.

Shayna slipped her cold hands into her coat pockets. The hard, unrelenting metal from the gun grazed her fingertips. She inched forward. "Are you going to let me in?"

He reared back. "I don't think this is a good time."

thirst

"Really?" Shayna asked. "And why is that?"

"We never get anywhere. I only agreed to talk in a counselor's office."

Counselor's office. What a joke! Why? To hear more lies, more denials. With a syrupy voice she said, "Please, honey, just let me in. I need to know there's still hope."

He glanced into the room. Her suspicions flared. "SHE's in there, isn't she?"

Their eyes met. Without warning, the slit in the door narrowed, and with a quick thrust, the door slammed tight, blocking her out, alone, in the cold. Suddenly, her options converged irrevocably, blindly.

Each time a shot cracked, shattering the quiet night, the gun jerked backwards, causing another wayward blast. The door splintered, the window shattered.

Moments later in a blur, she ran. Grass passed underfoot. She scrambled uphill, until, out of the blue, an iron weight rammed into her. Once decked, the lights went out.

~~~

At the police station, in a windowless room lit by a pulsating fluorescent tube, Shayna raised her fingers to her nose and breathed the thick, pungent scent of gunpowder. It smelled sweet and oddly comforting, like a cloud of smoke from a kid's cap gun. The memory dissolved when the keys rattled and the heavy metal door opened.

A man in a suit entered, extending his hand. "Mrs. Lutz, my name is Randall Curtis. Here's my card. I've come on behalf of your mother. She called and asked me to represent you in these proceedings."

His handshake was solid. Shayna asked, "How did she know?"

"Your husband called her."

"Jeremy? He's all right then?"

"Evidently. You're very lucky he didn't get hurt."

The man's starched blue collar dug into his neck. He continued, "First, we need to get you out of here. We'll have to go before the judge and tell him you're not a risk for flight and will abide by the order of protection. Is that doable?"

"Order of protection? That won't be necessary."

"I'm afraid you have no choice. "

"But the police took the gun."

"Mrs. Lutz, the gun's not the issue. Assault charges are pending. You must stay away from your husband and refrain from all contact until these issues are resolved."

"But if we can't communicate, how are we going to work on our marriage?"

"Unfortunately, I'm a lawyer, Mrs. Lutz, not a psychologist."

She looked into his uncomplicated face, clean shaven, wrinkle-free, devoid of the ravages of too much liquor or sun or worry. Her glance dropped to his left hand. "I see you're not married."

He stalled, then said, "But I am."

Shayna looked into his clear blue eyes. Was he telling the truth? "Then you should understand. Sometimes you have to fight for what's yours."

He nodded. "Yes, but fighting has rules, parameters."

So does marriage, she wanted to add.

"Your call, Mrs. Lutz," he said with an easy smile. "I'm here to help."

Her shoulders relaxed for the first time in weeks. "Okay, whatever you say," she agreed. "And please call me Shayna."

By daybreak she was back in her kitchen, frothing milk from their exported *espresso* machine. Through the curling steam and cigarette smoke she thought about men and their lies – like hell he was married.

Later that day, at 5:00 p.m., she parked across the street from her lawyer's office and began another vigil. Unlike previous evenings, her wait was quickly aborted as the heavy brass door sprung open. Remarkably, Mr. Randall Curtis continued to look unscathed, fresh, as if nothing had passed between them. But she knew otherwise.

This time her trek took a different path, not to the suburb but into the city, to a nicely appointed home in an upscale neighborhood. There he turned into a winding driveway that disappeared behind the house. She rolled into a parking spot, flipped down the mirror and checked her lipstick. She then got out of the car, stepped to the front door and pressed the doorbell.

thirst

He answered. His expectant face quickly froze. "What are you doing here?"

"I've come to meet HER."

"Her?" he said.

"Your wife. Where is SHE?" Shayna taunted.

Disbelief crept into his face. "You better leave," he said.

A dark-haired woman, too round and plain to be a true contender, sidled up behind him. "Honey, what's going on?"

"Get in the house," he said firmly, pushing her back.

Shayna's shock turned to giddiness. "What a porker."

From an inside pocket he pulled out a cell phone and pressed some digits. "This is an emergency, I have a woman here who's – "

Shayna smirked. "Surely, this isn't HER."

The piglet looked alarmed.

"Can I ask a rhetorical question?" Shayna said to the woman. "Do YOU squeal?"

~~~~~

Author's Note:

My longest sentence, a craft moment, is in this story. It follows, How did it happen? The sentence tumbled out practically whole. Regarding the last line. I took the collective advice of a writer's group and ended the piece a paragraph earlier, where there's some punch. In rewrite, it's not unusual for a narrative to start later and finish sooner. The Other Woman is a genre story

thirst

with an ending that hangs. I hope the lack of resolution highlights how, when not reeled in, obsession metastasizes. The Other Woman was first published in A Cruel World.

~ S o c k s ~

When my husband started wearing socks other than his usual white tubes and plain black knits, I began to wonder. Then when the socks went from discrete patterns to pastel argyles, I stressed out.

"Honey," I said at breakfast, glancing below the table. "What are those things?"

He pulled his chair away and wiggled his toes. "Why, they're yellow socks with golf clubs on them."

"But you don't golf."

He returned to the paper, languidly took a sip of coffee and said, "That's true."

As I went through the day, another thought cropped up, not only was he wearing the socks, but he was unabashedly entering a clothing store, pouring over the racks and making a conscious decision of which ones to buy. This coming from a man who rarely shopped was . . . well, disturbing. Then a sudden realization came over me – when a pattern changes (no pun intended), something had to be up. Another woman, was she buying them? I hadn't seen any receipts.

"Honey," I said the following morning (his feet d'jour now attired in, what appeared to be, some permutation of the confederate flag), "I'm not sure how practical these socks are."

"What do you mean?"

"You know what happens when you wash socks. Sooner or later one always gets lost. Before you know it, you'll have a drawer full of orphaned socks. In the long run, the expense will add up."

He gave a quick nod, then turned to read the nutritional information on the cereal box. "Wow," he said. "This stuff's filled with fiber."

I told him this to see his reaction. Would he defend himself? Did cheating husbands defend themselves? I had no idea.

Twenty-four hours later, sporting a checkerboard design with irregularly placed chessmen, he picked up the conversation from the day before. "Socks are never really lost in the wash," he said. "They're just stuck to other things, inside a pant leg, tangled up in a towel. It's no big deal."

Of course I already knew that.

Later, after he left for work, I went into his sock drawer. I wasn't sure what I'd find, maybe a love note. But it was worse

thirst

than I'd thought. He had expanded the sock space to two full drawers. Not only that, but all the socks, both new and freshly washed, were rolled neatly into tight cylinders, not unlike a tray of pigs-in-the-blanket, a neat cornucopia of descending colors, patterns. When had he become so obsessed? Then another thought, more disturbing than the first, came to mind – was he exploring his feminine side? I slammed the drawers shut.

At dinner, I put my foot down. "Honey, I think this sock thing is getting out of hand. You need to see someone."

He blinked and screwed up his face. "See someone? Like who?"

"A therapist."

"Don't think so," he said. "By the way, these mashed potatoes are very tasty."

After the evening news, I thumbed through the phone book. If he wasn't going to see a therapist, I had to. My world was unraveling.

The doctor looked remarkably like Freud. He was an older man with a beard and horn-rimmed glasses. The leather couch groaned when I settled in. After a brief interview, he said with a hint of a German accent, "You know it's not the socks. It's never the socks. It's life. It's the never-knowing. Why do we exist? Is there a reason?"

"My," I said, losing all hope. "Are you saying it's futile?"

"In general, yes, life is futile. But, my dear, you are lucky."

"I am?"

"In your case there may be an answer."

My breath caught. "Really? What is it?"

He stood up and bellowed. "Face him, woman! Demand an explanation!"

"Yes, yes" I said, rising from my misery. It was so obvious. I then wrote a check for one hundred and fifty dollars.

The following morning, I made buckwheat pancakes, his favorite. I even warmed the syrup. His socks were pale blue with green hovering seahorses. "Honey," I asked, "could you answer one simple question?"

He wiped his mouth with a paper napkin. "What is it?"

"Why do you have all these socks?"

He leaned back in the chair. "I thought you'd never ask."

The answer! I was about to hear the answer! My heart pounded.

He then eyed me with a sinister glint. "Why, you ask?" he said reaching across the table. "For the same reason you have all those shoes."

~~~~~

Author's Note:

I wrote "Socks" in two hours, from four in the morning until six, a personal record. The creative process – is it simply a function of the individual brain or something more, something greater? From a craft perspective, this story helped me hone my transition skills. For some reason seamlessly skipping time or moving from one scene to another has often confounded me. There are many

thirst

tricks, sleights of pen. The more I practice, the easier it becomes. "Socks" features two relatively well-adjusted adults, a refreshing departure. Socks was first published in Zimmer-zine.

~ J a c k ~

It began with a simple drive-by into the old neighborhood.
An afterthought mostly. Jack had three hours to burn before the
meeting at the airport and decided to swing over to the north
end and check out the old house, school and whatever vestiges
remained after forty-odd years. He thought it would be interesting
but fleeting. Nothing that would affect him in any significant way. A
previously seen movie, a rerun, floating by with occasional bits of
recollection. Entertainment. He wasn't a man to live in the past.

He couldn't say he had grown up in Buffalo or any other place
for that matter. His father was always on the run from jobs, bill
collectors and the occasional female. But of all the places they'd
stayed, Buffalo was the longest. Almost three years, sometime
between the fifth and eighth grades in a neighborhood better
than most, or so he recalled.

thirst

The way there wasn't certain. He had to get to Main Street, Route 5, the primary thoroughfare that cut the city in half. That much he knew. And since he was a salesman who traveled, who had seen most of the country, who had a natural ability to find just about any street in any city, he jumped on the expressway and headed west.

In record time, he came upon Main Street, along with the University, but one milestone seemed missing – the viaduct. What had been a deep dip beneath a railroad line was now an open road, flat as a pancake. He and his friends, Lou and Dan, had spent hours up high, near the tracks smoking cigarettes and drinking beer or wine or whatever else they could steal from their parents' homes. Yes, now he remembered. He drank so much *crème de menthe* one time that his shit'd turned green. How had he forgotten that? To this day, he couldn't eat anything mint, no mouthwash or candy or ice cream. It turned his stomach.

Not too far away would be the house. He made a right on Woodbridge, another on Parker, then slowed down. He had lived in a double, upstairs. The owner lived downstairs, an old spinster who often complained to his father about the noise he and his friends made after school, listening to music or having the TV too loud. But later in the week, she'd bring up cookies, freshly baked, and he'd try to be quiet, at least for a couple of days. And he now wondered how old that woman actually was. It wasn't uncommon for his father to go downstairs to change a lightbulb or unclog a drain and not come back until the eleven o'clock news.

74

thirst

He pulled over. The old gray house was painted hunter green. It was an ordinary clapboard house, close to the street with no distinguishing features. For a moment, he tried to make some connection between the past and the present, between the boy he was and the man he'd become. Perhaps something he could use in his job, an anecdote that would link his formative years with the selling of insurance.

He inched the car forward and looked down the walkway that ran into the backyard. The concrete slabs heaved, and now that he was older, he understood why. In the winter, icicles had hung from gutters and dripped frigid drops onto the crown of his head. "Watch out for those suckers," his father'd said. "They'll spike right through you." Clearly, the years of snow and ice and water had taken their toll. He considered taking that walk again, along the side of the house. But it was only a measly couple of yards. What would be the point?

A few minutes later, he went by the school. It was smaller than he remembered, and remarkably transformed into condominiums, ghosts of classrooms now used as kitchens and bathrooms and bedrooms. What the hell did they do with the cavernous halls, the lockers, the principal's office where he often sat looking at his reflection in the bookcase glass? Gutted, of course. Reconfigured. Time moved on.

He coasted down a few more streets. First, by Lou's house, which he couldn't quite discern, then by Dan's, queerly painted in pinks and purples. Where were they now? Had they made it out of the sixties alive? Whatever. They probably wouldn't have anything in common at this point in the game.

The block emptied out onto Hertel. He was about to head back when he noticed the *Swimming Pool* sign. He checked his watch and instead of turning right, headed up the dead end street where, he thought, it curved into the pool and park. His memory served him well. He pulled into a parking spot and got out of the car.

The pool hadn't yet been open for the season. The diving boards weren't up. He walked down an incline into the park. Like everything else, the area was small and inconsequential – a baseball field, handball court, some swings and slides. Over at the playground, mothers with empty strollers watched kids who were running around in circles. With plenty of time, he picked a bench by the baseball diamond, sat, and closed his eyes in the late morning sun. A mother yelled, a child cried. How clear their voices carried.

The last time he'd been in this park was in the evening. He and Dan and Lou were drinking, cutting up by the horses on springs. They even had a joint, when a girl walked by, taking a short cut through the park. A girl, Dan knew from the neighborhood. She joined them and drank a little beer, and before long she showed them things in the moonlight for another sip or drag. Kid's stuff. Until things got weird. Dares were made and the girl was half-naked. They were just kids back then, Jack thought, with bodies they didn't understand. Dan held her down. First, for Lou then for Jack. When it was Dan's turn, it took two of them to keep her from screaming.

On the way back to the car, Jack pulls out his cell phone and dials home. His thirteen-year-old daughter answers. He wants to make sure she's home, she's okay. She's chewing gum and irritated by him and by his probing questions. After they hang up, he sighs, relieved. So far she's safe. Or so he thinks.

~~~~~

Author's Note:

"Jack" is the second of two dark stories in this collection. I usually write grim stories from an understated, unemotional perspective. The quietness, I think, makes them feel real, and ironically, more powerful. I thought a lot about Jack and who he might be. My general sense is that he's a regular guy who may be living next door or sitting close by. There's a saying that revenge is best served cold. In "Jack" retribution is served with a twist of irony.

~ T h e   C u r e ~

The view from the 10th floor seemed to make me dizzy, or was it the stifling heat? Whatever the reason, I pulled open my purse and dug out some gum. Perhaps I was just nervous and needed something to chew.

"Sure you don't want any coffee?" Giselle called out. She was off in another room, slamming cupboards.

I should have broken the news the minute she opened the door, but her reaction to seeing me was unexpected. She gave me a hug.

"No, I'm fine. Thanks."

"Okey-dokey," she said. "Be there in a sec."

"Take your time," I said trying to sound blasé as if it were a casual visit, a simple stop-by, how-ya-doin'. But certainly she had to be curious. We hadn't had any contact in years. Granted, time accelerated with age, but she'd acted as if we had just spoken.

I stepped away from the window and looked around the living room. Nothing was familiar. Not surprising. The last time I'd seen Giselle was in her other home, the one she and her husband had lived in for most of their married life. Still, I was curious if there'd be something recognizable, some token of our shared past, a photograph perhaps, or some memento forgotten. I walked to the china cabinet. Stemware gleamed behind the glass.

I first met Giselle at Oliver's, an upscale restaurant with intimate tables tucked in dark alcoves. She had very red lips that left clear marks on the rim of the champagne glass. Her signature scent, I found out later, was White Linen, a crisp, clean smell with a hint of complication. Her fingernails were lacquered, red with half moons showing. And of course she was wearing The Ring, an emerald-cut two carat diamond that my father'd given her. A ring that now sat in a tufted row in my jewelry box. A ring I would never wear.

"Sure I can't get you a cup of coffee? How about some tea or a glass of juice?"

"No thanks."

For the last twenty-four hours I had debated about making contact. I could have told my father that I couldn't reach her and left it at that. But given the circumstances, I just couldn't lie.

Her disembodied voice continued to ramble. "It's so nice to see you. I love surprises."

Yes, Giselle was never one to plan. A characteristic my father had loved, then paid the price for.

"Nice place," I said to the air around me.

A small curio cabinet, filled with knock-off Faberge eggs, hung on the wall. Intricately adorned in rich enamel colors, they were ridiculously gaudy and purposeless.

"So you've found my weakness."

I turned. She was carrying a silver tray of cookies. "Most of them are from trips. In fact, your father and I picked up the green one when we were in Austria." She placed the tray down and got a faraway look. "Now what year was that?"

I nodded politely. Trip to Vienna. I couldn't remember the year, but my parents were still married at the time. As was she.

She walked over. "85 maybe. I don't travel much now. The world comes to me. I shop online. Ebay."

Standing beside me, I was struck how small she was, shorter, thinner in every way, even the strands of her blond hair were sparse and brittle looking. Her boney hand reached out for mine. "Come sit down."

The couch cushion gave away easily. I sank low. "You're probably wondering why I'm here."

She reached for the cookies. "It's so nice to have company. Please have one."

"No thanks." Was she listening? "It's about my father."

"Your father?"

thirst

"He asked me to speak with you. I tried calling, but your number's unlisted."

"Unlisted? Yes, I had to stop all those salesmen. Imagine trying to sell me a timeshare or a mortgage . . . And how is Joe?"

"Not good I'm afraid. He's in the hospital."

She reared back and put her hand to her mouth. "No. Not Joe. Oh, Mindy, I'm so sorry. Here I'm going on. What's wrong?"

"He had heart surgery last week. A triple bypass. But there's a problem, an infection of some kind. He's not responding to the antibiotics. He wants to see you."

"Me? He wants to see me?"

"Giselle, I totally understand if you don't want – "

"But of course I'll visit. What hospital is he in?"

"The General. I could take you."

"Would you? When were you thinking?"

"Tomorrow evening. After I get out of work. Say six-thirty."

She looked off for a moment. "Yes. That sounds fine."

Suddenly, I'm relieved. Since my mother only visited during the day, the logistics of keeping the two women apart wouldn't be a problem. Not that it ultimately mattered. The parties involved – my father, mother and Giselle – were all free agents, divorced and footloose for over a decade.

I reached for a cookie, then took a bite. The gum I'd been chewing disintegrated instantly. I swallowed hard, and half-listened as Giselle rambled on about her two sons and several

82

grandchildren. Remarkably, for the next ten minutes the nightmare of my father's surgery receded. I had another cookie.

At work the next day, my cell rang. It was my mother. "Mindy, I went to see your father today. Guess who showed up?"

My mother's social life had suddenly blossomed now that Dad was hospitalized. The news was out and old friends had been setting up tag team vigils. "Who?"

"That woman."

My breath caught. Giselle? But that wasn't possible. I kept calm. "Mother, what woman?"

"Giselle! Giselle!"

"Oh."

"You don't seem surprised."

"Well – "

"She's very skinny and much older than I pictured. Who knew? My God, I could blow the woman over."

"Did she say what she was doing there?"

"Your father said he wanted to see her. Do you believe it?"

"How is Dad?"

"I'm afraid not good, sweetie. The whole time we were there, all kinds of things were going off. I guess his blood pressure spiked."

"My God."

"Now Mindy don't get upset. They calmed him down. Anyway, Giselle and I went to lunch at the hospital cafeteria."

I collapsed into the chair. "You went to lunch together?"

"Yes. You know the hospital has really good food and very reasonable. I had the gumbo. It was delicious. Anyway, Giselle and I decided we needed to be practical. So we talked about the expenses, you know, for the funeral."

"Mother!"

"Mindy, please. Let me finish. I don't think your father has life insurance. Burials run around six thousand dollars. We were thinking about that engagement ring. Maybe it could be used as a down payment. I mean you're never going to wear it. Giselle thought – "

I'd just entered la-la land. "Mother," I interrupted, "I gotta go to the hospital."

"But you're at work."

"You're scaring me. I'm worried about Dad."

"Now, Mindy, calm down. He's in God's hands."

By the time I reached the hospital, I was sweating profusely. When I got off the elevator, the ward nurse said, "So you've heard."

Heard? I hadn't heard anything and didn't want to hear anything. I barreled past her. The door to his room was closed. I figured the worse – they must be scrubbing the place down. I tore in.

"Hi, honey," my father said. He was sitting up.

"Dad?"

"Come on in. Want this Jell-O?"

The room. Something was missing – the IV pole.

84

thirst

"You're eating?"

"Starved."

"So, the antibiotics kicked in."

He shrugged. "I guess."

I couldn't believe the change. His color was back, his voice was strong. "That's great, Dad."

He nodded, then slurped some soup.

"Mom called me. Told me Giselle was here. I was supposed to bring her after I got out of work."

"Mmm."

"Did she say anything?"

He wiped his lips. "Who?"

"Giselle."

"Yeah, she said something about wanting to see me as soon as she found out. I think she thought I was gonna croak."

"I guess I won't have to bring her later."

"Don't think so."

I sat in the only chair. "How strange having them both here."

"You can say that again."

I recalled what my mother'd said about his blood pressure. "Must have been upsetting."

My father leaned back against the pillow and sucked his teeth. "Here I was flat on my back, feeling like crap. The minute Giselle peeked into the room, I thought fur was gonna fly. That's when everything started going off, and I coded."

"WHAT?"

85

"Mindy, calm down. I'm all right."

"You coded in front of them? Mom didn't say anything about that."

"This place was like Grand Central. They stripped me down and shot me up with something. Then they used one of those heart starters."

"Dad, how awful."

"At some point I must have passed out because I was lying on my back looking up at the sky. Buzzards were circling. That's when I heard them talking about the weather, the temperature, how sunny it was."

"Who was talking?"

"Your mother and Giselle."

"So they were in your dream?"

"Dream? Hell, no. In the middle of everything, I opened my eyes. They were standing right over there." He pointed to spot by the wall. "They were talking about the weather, about having lunch. That's when I had a moment of clarity . . . " He dug into a mound of mashed potatoes. "Mindy, both those women put me through the wringer, and now that I was about to check out, they were going to be one big happy family."

It was a curious take on my father's affair and all that followed. He filled his mouth and mumbled. "Over my dead body. You know?"

thirst

For the first time in weeks, I felt lighter. Then something truly remarkable happened. I floated over to my father's side. "Yeah, Dad, screw them."

~~~~~

Author's Note:

The hospital scene of a dying man and two women had been bouncing around in my head for years. A lifetime of stories could be told from this set-up, endlessly unique and intriguing. I am of the opinion that no two stories are alike, despite theme, despite archetypes. In the "Cure" I took an inspirational turn and chose the POV of yet a third person. Still, I have not abandoned the idea of telling a multiple POV story from one scene, one setting. In fact, I already have the title, "Florence and Normandy."

~ J e a l o u s y ~

"Too busy," you'd said.

I wondered.

So I drove by your house. Your car was in the drive, along with hers, that rusted-out sedan. Not bothering to knock, I climbed the stairs. Moans echoed down the hallway. Before leaving, I blew out the pilot and turned on the gas.

~~~~~

Author's Note:

How short can a short story be? Pretty short. Jealousy is fifty words. To read more fifty- word stories, visit, www.tangents. co.uk/50words. Jealousy was first published by Tangents.

~ D e a r D r. R i c e ~

For a brief moment during his lunch hour, Myron felt relieved from the threat of terrorism. It occurred while eating a cheese and pepperoni hot pocket. Condoleezza Rice was on television. Her name was spelled beneath her talking head. He thought it was overextended, not the talking head, but the name, and definitively convoluted. Condoleezza herself was another anomaly, not only a woman and black and Republican but curiously cute and somewhat childlike only with a razor-sharp brain and powerful voice. The woman, he decided between sips of Dr. Pepper, was capable, but could she be trusted? He then wondered where she'd been on September 11th. Most likely in the same bunker with the old boy network. In a flash, he discounted her and wiped his mouth with a paper napkin. And by the time the noon

91

news moved onto the weather, Myron returned to thinking about terrorism and how he could possibly survive it.

A week previous to watching Dr. Rice, Myron had spent seventy-two hours in observation at a psychiatric emergency room. He had been admitted after he was found ministering to those who'd listen at Wal-Mart the prophetic words of Jim Morrison, "No one gets out alive." He truly meant it as consolation (everyone has to die sometime), but no one wanted to take any chances. The bulge in his back pocket could have been plastic explosives, not the flashlight he had absentmindedly placed there after his hands were full with a hefty box of cornflakes, batteries, toaster, and he didn't want to make a trip to the front of the store for a cart.

At the time, being hospitalized was a welcomed relief since the terror alert had risen to red for no apparent reason. It was neither the eleventh of the month nor a holiday. For three days he finally got some sleep, possibly from the Risperdal, possibly from his expectation that hospitals usually seemed off limits even for terrorists. But now back at work, his general anxiety was escalating, for good reason. Not only did he take the subway to his job, but he also worked in the mail room. This amounted to nine hours of high risk behavior per day. If a bomb on the subway didn't get him, the anthrax, sarin gas, small pox would.

Of course, he had come up with some pre-emptive safeguards. At work, he now wore latex gloves, but the wearing of surgical masks, which he had purchased in bulk at a prohibitive cost to himself, was denied by the powers that be, stating that it showed a general lack of confidence in the company as well as all governing units, including the CIA, FBI, and the ubiquitous Department of Homeland Security. Besides, he was told by Barnes, his supervisor's supervisor, they were all soldiers against the war, and he was an American, and he should stand proud, fearless . . . yada, yada.

In any event, Myron made accommodations the best he could. At his work station, he devised a shield made of plexiglass that sat atop two concrete blocks, beneath which he was able to open envelopes in clear view and which provided a barrier of sorts, giving him at least a few seconds of lead time before any cloud of white or gray or brown powder dissipated among the molecules of air.

The subway was another matter. From home to work was eleven miles (a rough calculation using MapQuest) which amounted to a white-knuckled seven-minute ride each way. Myron's ability to control this environment was compromised due to the innumerable variables that so many people of so many colors with so many agendas could present. Still, he was not totally defenseless. In his backpack, which he now carried everywhere, was an Israeli-issued gas mask, pepper spray and a roll of heavy-duty duct tape. The gas mask and pepper spray were no-brainers. The duct tape. Well, maybe he'd have to secure an area or stop the bleeding.

thirst

When he returned to his work space, located in the corner of the mail room, there was a message scribbled on a yellow sticky note attached to the back of his chair. *See me, Barnes.* After he read the note, he looked up. His co-workers, Rico and Lenny, abruptly turned away. Myron smiled. "Not a problem, guys. Got it covered."

"How you doing today, Myron?" Barnes said five minutes later. They were sitting across from each other. Barnes's desk had a cleared, shiny glass top. Myron wasn't sure what Barnes did, what role he played, what service he provided.

"Pretty good and yourself?"

Barnes nodded. "You're feeling okay then?"

Myron shrugged. "Yeah. Why do you ask?"

"Well, you took off a few days ago."

"I'm fine. Thanks for asking."

An executive pen set with a marble base sat in front of Barnes. He pulled one of the pens out, then rolled its shaft between his fingers.

If you had asked Myron, this was not unusual behavior for Barnes. His boss's boss never seemed to be totally present.

Myron reminded Barnes. "You wanted to see me?"

Barnes slid the pen into its holder. "Yes, Myron. It's about your workstation. I'm afraid it's not acceptable."

"Not acceptable? In what way?"

Barnes leaned forward. "Myron, we've talked about this. Do you really think that contraption's going to help? Lord, it took

94

months to clean up the Post Office and Congress buildings. Whatever's going to happen – "

Myron stopped him. "Excuse me, Mr. Barnes, but I have another idea. I need to do some research but I think I may be onto something. You know those canaries they put in mines? Well, maybe goldfish or some kind of insect, like ants can be used. This is my thought. I open a package, powder comes out and I immediately put it into water or something contained like an ant farm."

Barnes raised his hands. "Myron, stop it. No more ideas. Let me get to the point. Who's the terrorist in this place?"

Myron thought. There was this commuter guy, a recent graduate from Case Western. Came from Sri Lanka. Not that he'd cast aspersions. "Terrorist? Here?"

"Who's scaring everyone? Who's stirring the pot? Myron, who recently got arrested at Wal-Mart?"

Clearly, this wasn't a trick question. "But Mr. Barnes, I wasn't arrested. Besides, I'm the good guy. I'm trying to save people."

"Myron, the company is worried about you."

The company worried? How was that possible? Only people worried.

"Myron, we have to let you go. For your own good, you understand."

"You're firing me?"

"No, of course not. We're just concerned for you, your health, your well-being."

thirst

"But I've been here ten years. You – "

"Of course we'll highly recommend you and not mention any health issues. You have my word on that. Now I've negotiated a nice severance package. One month's salary. And you'll be eligible for unemployment and covered by Cobra on your health insurance." Barnes stood. "Myron, I'm very excited for you. You're entering a new chapter in your life." He reached out his hand. "Thanks for coming up."

Myron didn't remember how he got back to the mail room.

It was Rico who came over first. "You okay?"

"I just got canned."

"Myron, you can't let them do this to you. We need you here. "

Lenny walked up behind Rico. He had a slip of paper in his hand. "You gotta see Kinta."

"Kinta?"

"She's a kick-ass lawyer. She'll know what to do."

~~~

"The Constitution sucks, totally anachronistic. Now the Bill of Rights, that's a document." Kinta was sitting behind a stack of files. A ragged, half-eaten sandwich was in front of her. Mayonnaise and crumbs left grease spots on one of the manila folders. She took a bite. "So how much money do you want?" she mumbled.

Myron had been confused from the moment he'd met Kinta, a petite black woman with an unruly head of hair. This question was equally obscure. "Aren't I supposed to pay you?"

She laughed. "You're a character, Myron. No offense. We're goin' in. How about a million?"

"A million dollars?"

"Of course dollars. Granted Euros would be better. Man, that European market is solid, but when in Rome. My commission will come out of the million. Say twenty-five percent when we settle. And we WILL settle."

Myron liked it when she said 'we', made him feel part of something.

"So. What do you say?"

"I just want my job back."

"Excuse me?"

"I need to work."

"Myron, Myron." She leaned back in the chair. "In life, on rare occasions, a golden opportunity comes a'knockin'. Your employer, Mr. Barnes, has indeed granted you a new chapter. Unfortunately for him, it's on his nickel. He has violated not only your right to free speech, but has shown bias, failed to show cause and denied you due process. These infringements on the Fifth and Fourteenth Amendments as well as his clear, flagrant revilement of the ADA means you got a blank check coming your way. Heck. Let's double it and go in for two million."

"But I like my job."

"What about terrorism, and the mail, and your ride into work? You won't have to worry about it anymore. Well, at least not that kind of terrorism."

"There's another kind of terrorism?"

"Myron, compare the odds, being blown up by some lunatic with a beer belly of plastic explosives or getting walloped by the Big C."

"Big C?"

"Cancer. Now that's terrorism. It's random and scares the crap out of people. And once diagnosed is it ever out of your mind? Does a day go by that you aren't trolling Google for some breakthrough, some new extract from the rain forest that will zap it out of you?"

"Good point."

"Hmm . . . But I digress. Even though we won't be going to court, it still may take awhile, a year or two. You'll probably have to find another job in the interim, unless you've got some money put aside."

Myron shook his head. "I got nothing."

Abruptly, Kinta stood and held out her hand. "You're a good person, Myron. And before long you'll be a rich good person. A rarity indeed. I'll be in touch."

Myron's meeting with Kinta made him feel worse. He was over his head, no job, no money, with growing concern about his health. He spent the rest of the day at the library. By the time he finished a number of Google searches, he had a splitting headache, felt some left-sided weakness and couldn't see too well.

On his last day of work, Myron found a second note from Barnes. Rico and Lenny told him to throw it in the trash. But before he made the mail deliveries, Myron stopped upstairs.

"Myron," Barnes said, "so you went to see a lawyer."

Myron shrugged.

"Kunta Kinte somebody."

"Her name's Kinta."

He nodded. "Whatever. Anyway, I've talked to the Board about you and we decided to give you another chance."

"Chance?"

"To keep your job."

"I don't understand what you mean by 'chance'. Sounds kind of temporary. Will I be on probation or something?"

"No, of course not. It was a poor choice of words. You can keep your job."

"What about my workstation? Do I have to make any changes?"

"No problem as long as it doesn't affect your job performance."

Myron wasn't quite certain, but he seemed to have the upper hand. He needed to test the waters. "Will I be getting a raise?"

"Raise? How much of a raise?"

Myron thought fast. "Double."

Barnes reared back. "Double? Now just hold on . . .

Myron stopped paying attention. He looked out the window to the river. The current sparkled. He had never noticed.

"Myron, are you listening? How about a fifty percent increase?"

"Sounds good."

It was settled. Myron agreed to keep his job and went on a payment plan with Kinta. She only asked for two thousand. He remained concerned about terrorism, but diversified. Every Friday, when he delivered the mail, he included handouts on the warning signs of various diseases. By Christmas, Barnes was diagnosed with prostate cancer. They caught it early, thanks to Myron. And the next time Myron saw Dr. Rice on television, he decided to pass along some information on lymphoma. With a clean sheet of paper he began, *Dear Dr. Rice . . .*

~~~~~

Author's Note:

Ah, the beauty of closure. An epilogue is the tidy bow disdained by editors and loved by readers. From a writer's perspective, it's a terrific way to end a story cleanly and quickly. Another craft point, often scorned by yours truly, is the clear distinction between my voice and that of Myron's. Would he use such words as convoluted, discounted, pre-emptive? Probably not. On the other hand, I argue with myself, many PHDs drive cabs. "Dear Dr. Rice" is about the good, the bad, the sane, the crazed and how we are all in this together. I love Myron. He should run for vice-president. As for president . . . Kinta. Dear Dr. Rice was first published in Unlikely Stories.

~ T e d d y B e a r ~

At 11 a.m. Sunday, Ted Blaine sat in the alcove of his rented room. The chores for the week – laundry, shopping, changing the sheets – had been dealt with, leaving only one distasteful task: the dreaded weekly visit from his sister, Meg. As the water boiled, he reached for a package of store-bought cookies, ripped it open, then moved the plastic tray next to her waiting cup. He figured the more he prepared for the visit, the faster she'd be in and out. Never really worked.

He looked out the window and down to the street. The spot where she parked her Cavalier remained empty. His eyes ran up the road. Nothing moved, not a soul, not a car. God, he despised Sunday, the lifelessness of it. He scoured for signs of life, perhaps a shadow or the glow of a lit cigarette amid the dark windows and unevenly pulled blinds of the weathered brick building across the street. But the desolation continued. His glance finally settled on, what appeared to be, piles of coal along the street. Of course the craggy mounds were just exhaust-encrusted snow. Ted shook his head. This hapless view was nothing compared the sequin waters of St. Petersburg. Damn. Instead of returning home to Buffalo, he should have gone west. But then again, wounded animals tended to head for familiar territory.

He sighed and turned his attention back into the room. The door to the bathroom was cracked open. Deep inside his chest he felt the familiar ache – Stacy. What he missed most was her rinsed-out lingerie on the shower curtain rod. What he missed least were her lame excuses for not coming home, two, three days at a time. Leaning forward, he reached for his wallet. He had made promises (often broken) to limit the times he'd indulge. But it was Sunday and the morning had gone by with hardly a thought of her.

Tucked behind his driver's license was her picture, naked in bed, lying on her side, her head propped in a folded elbow. He ran his finger across the tacky, creased surface. In a drugstore checkout somewhere in Tennessee, they had picked up the Polaroid. She liked having her picture taken. Before snapping the shutter, he'd lingered. "Come on, Teddy Bear," she'd mumbled through a forced smile. "Take the damn picture." But he took his sweet time. It was only through the viewfinder that he'd have her singular attention, feel a modicum of control, however fleeting.

In the distance a car door slammed. Ted leaned forward and peered out the window. Meg's solid, squat figure, clothed in a heavy black coat, stepped off the street and onto the sidewalk.

Ted gave the photograph another longing gaze. He followed the curves, the way her body dipped and rose, finally feasting on those full breasts with dark nipples. His calloused hands, she'd said, drove her crazy. Well, now it was his turn to be driven to the edge. Fifteen months and he was still stuck, mired in a lovesick maze, where all his thoughts twisted, turned and backtracked to the six months they had together.

He shook his head. Meg had told him the best way to forget Stacy was to move on, find someone else. There were a couple of candidates – the landlady downstairs and Jennie at the hardware store, both nice girls, not particularly youthful, but nice nevertheless. Ted now thought of another drawback of having been with Stacy. Besides having to deal with her disappearing acts, he seemed hopelessly stuck on youngish women. Damn fool, he told himself. But would he have changed a moment? Simply – no.

Hearing Meg's familiar steps, he buried the picture in his wallet and went for the door.

"Effing weather," said Meg in the open doorway, stomping her feet on the small rubber mat. "Every year, I swear I'll leave. And look at me, look at us. What are we, masochists?"

Ted didn't want to be part of the editorial "we," but let it go. With Meg, he had to pick his battles. He extended his hands.

"Winter won't last much longer. Give me your coat. I'll hang it up."

She slipped her arms from the sleeves. "Don't bother." She gave the coat a heave-ho and tossed it onto the bed. Then, straightening her sweater, she walked to the table and sat. "Chocolate chips today. Are they the chewy kind?"

"There's a difference?"

"Of course." She lowered her head and zeroed in. "Usually the thinner they are, the chewier." Her face scrunched up. "They look pretty thick. Bet they're like rocks."

"Sorry," he said.

"Don't be sorry," she said with a wave of her hand. "They're still good for dunking."

Ted glanced at the bedside clock. She usually stayed a half hour. From his quick calculation, only thirty seconds had gone by. God, how did this ritual begin? Yes, now he remembered. The first month back home, he was, what was her word? Despondent.

"How was work this week?" she asked.

"Fine."

"Meet anybody?"

Ted put a teaspoon of instant coffee into her cup. "I met plenty of people. That's my job."

"Ted, you know what I mean. Any prospects?"

"No, Meg, no prospects. How about yourself?"

Her shoulders slumped. "Remember Jerry, the man who sang in the choir. He seemed interested, then poof, disappeared. I asked the Reverend about him. Apparently, the guy moved to Mt. Morris, wherever the hell that is." She picked up a cookie and held it in the air. "Let's face it, Ted. We Blaines are cursed. No way around it." She then took a bite. "Dry but tasty."

He sloshed hot water into her cup, then pushed the sugar and milk in front of her.

"Thanks," she said. "You okay?"

"I'm a big boy," he said in a level tone. "Stop worrying about me."

"Well, you certainly landed on your feet."

Sitting down, Ted stifled an ironic laugh. Here he was fifty-seven years old in a rented room with a job that paid minimal wage and unpaid bills up the wazoo. "I certainly did."

"Have you thought any more about getting a divorce?"

"Meg, let's not talk about that. Let's have a nice visit."

"Now Teddy – "

He interrupted, "Please don't call me Teddy." He was three years older for chrissake.

She settled back in the chair. "Well, all right. It's just that I've been thinking. In fact, I've got the perfect solution."

"Solution to what?"

"Your life."

He took a deep breath, thinking of the bottle of whiskey he kept in the cabinet below the sink. He could drink it or simply

thirst

creep up from behind and break it on her head. "Meg, any discussion about my life is off limits."

"It's not only about you. It's about us. Please listen."

He rolled his eyes, but kept quiet.

"I think we should pool our resources and move in together."

His mind seized up. "You're joking, right?"

"Joking? Of course not. We could buy a double. I'd prefer the downstairs, but we could negotiate – Why are you shaking your head?"

"I'm shaking my head because words escape me."

"Oh. Anyway, we're not getting any younger. We can help each other out. I can food shop, fix dinner. You can take care of the outside, do any repairs that come up. And of course this doesn't preclude either one of us from marrying again. We'll each have a flat. And, you'll like this, it would be cheaper. What are you paying here? Seventy-five a week. That's three hundred a month. Pooling our money, we might be able to upgrade, live in the suburbs. There's a really nice place next to Marge's. You remember Marge . . . ."

Her eyes sparkled. She was on a roll. Ted stopped listening, tuned out.

Stacy and he had lived in a motel for six months. They had looked at apartments, but he liked the smallness of the motel room, the intimacy. She was never more than a few steps away, doing the stuff women did – painting toenails, trying on clothes, showering in a steamy haze.

106

"There's only one snag. Ted, are you listening?"

"Yes. And what's that?"

"Now don't get bent out of shape, but if you're still married, she'd be entitled to the property. We can't let that happen."

Remarkably, a trap door opened. He nodded. "Absolutely."

Her face lit up. "So you like the idea?"

"Meg, it's terrific. But like you said, until I'm divorced it's out of the question. But a divorce costs money. Money I don't have."

"I'll stake you."

"I can't take your money, Meg."

"You can pay me back. We'll consider it a loan."

"I'm in too much debt as it is." His mind raced with other arguments. "I gotta get myself situated. Besides weren't you talking about getting a condo? Houses can be expensive. We both know that."

She stared off. "Yes, that's true, but – "

"But what?"

She gave him a solemn look, stone-like. "Ted, she's out there."

"Who's out where?"

"That woman, that Stacy."

Ted raised his hands. "We agreed not to talk about her."

"But as long as you're married, her bills are yours. Aren't you taking a bigger chance by staying married than finally ending it? She already sent you that credit card bill. How many more will follow? How can you be sure she's not charging her way across the planet?"

Ted felt he was up against a wall with a firing squad taking potshots. That's how his sister made him feel, cornered, helpless, with no exit. Trying to remain calm, he ignored her and looked out the window.

"Don't have any answers, do you Ted? Always in denial. I don't know why I bother."

The fuse was now lit. Feeling a slight burn, he challenged her gaze. "Bother Meg? Bother with what?"

"With coming here every Sunday, trying to cheer you up. You know I could be doing other things. Takes almost two hours out of my day, my day off mind you. And for what, to see you moping around? Sometimes, I think you want to get back with that slut."

"Don't call her that," he said.

"Slut's being nice."

"I think you should leave."

"You're throwing me out?" She hauled herself from the chair. "Fine. I'm going. But not before I say one more thing. Don't you roll your eyes at me."

Ted got up, took the half-filled cups to the sink, and turned on the tap. As the sink filled with water, he squeezed in some dish detergent. To calm down, he focused on the billowing foam and began to count.

She was behind him, hovering. "It's over Ted. Get a life. That whore certainly has." Suddenly, the cookies he had bought sailed past him and splashed into the water. "Ha," she added, "Now it's your turn to clean up MY mess. Have fun." Seconds later the walls shook from the slamming door.

Like wreckage from a ship, cookies bobbed in the water. Ted reached in. Scalding his fingers, he grabbed the plastic tray and lifted it out. An idea struck. The molded compartment could be recycled, maybe used to hold sponges or soap. And for the first time that day, he smiled. Sundays were now officially his, to do as he pleased.

~~~

By midweek, Ted still hadn't filled the unexpected, but welcomed void, left by his sister. However, on Saturday afternoon an opportunity presented itself. During a breather at the hardware store, while sitting at the cash register, his eyes fell on Jennie. At that particular moment she was down the plumbing aisle sizing up plungers. Earlier in the day she had asked him about her bathtub drain. He had given her his opinion but now wondered if he should take to another level.

Ted watched as she moved, slightly slumped in jeans and a sweater. Jennie, middle-aged, was nothing like Stacy and Ted wasn't sure if he could make the transition, go from surf 'n' turf to macaroni 'n' cheese. Still, Jennie was not without charm. She smiled plenty and, no matter what the weather, seemed always upbeat. Compared with Stacy's moodiness and incessant whining, Jennie's personality was liquid sunshine.

Jennie turned toward him, holding up a gizmo that looked like a cross between an air pump and a plunger. It was an ingenious invention that coupled air pressure with suction, but besides being expensive, it was cumbersome to maneuver. He got off the stool and walked down the aisle.

"Listen, Jennie." He pulled out a heavy duty plunger. "Don't spend the extra money. This will do the job."

She bit the inside of her cheek. "I don't know, Ted. I already have one of those. It doesn't seem to work."

He turned the plunger upside down. "Not all plungers are created equal." He showed her the underside, where the molded rubber bottom folded into itself. "Bet yours is one of those single-edged ones. They're worthless. But this baby here. Well, if you want suction, you got it." Once the words were out, he felt heated, partly from embarrassment, partly from he wasn't sure what.

Her eyes twinkled. "That's what I need all right."

He blurted, "Listen, if you can give me a lift, maybe I could stop by tomorrow and give you a hand."

She smiled. "Sounds great. What time should I pick you up?"

"Tomorrow morning. Say around eleven?"

"Sure thing," she said.

Suddenly, Ted had a date of sorts.

As the shift wore on, he avoided her and by the time he left for the day, he felt vaguely remorseful. After all, he was still a married man. But that was only part of it. Bottom line was, and as Meg had deduced, he was still holding out for Stacy. However, later that evening, unwinding from the work week at the corner tavern, he calmed down. He was unplugging the woman's drain, for chrissake. Nothing more.

At 10:30 p.m. he returned to the rooming house. Betsy, the landlady, was waiting. "You have a visitor." She leaned toward him. "A woman."

Ted immediately thought of Meg. What had he done now?

"Says she's your wife."

Everything seemed to slant. He teetered toward the wall. "My wife?" he echoed.

"I asked for ID. It said Blaine." Her eyes darted up the stairs. "She's waiting."

Ted looked to the second floor.

"Now Ted, you've been a fine tenant, but it's one room per person. If she stays, I'll have to charge you double."

He nodded distractedly. "Not a problem."

By the time he reached the landing, he was winded. He stalled for a moment, not sure if he should knock. Instead, he ran his hand through his hair, stood straighter and turned the knob.

The only light came from the bathroom. It cast a yellow slice onto the carpet. "Teddy Bear," came her sultry voice. "I've been waiting."

He saw her silhouette in the bay window, sitting where Meg had sat.

"Stacy?"

thirst

She didn't get up. "It's me, baby. Been awhile, huh?"

He reached for the pole lamp located next to the dresser and fumbled with the tiny ribbed cap. Suddenly the room filled with soft light. She was wearing one of his T-shirts, the wife beater kind she had called them. Her breasts bulged out from the top and sides, stretching the fabric to transparency. Her tits, like pebbles, looked as if they'd split the material altogether. Her bare legs were crossed. Given past history, he doubted she was wearing anything else.

Planted to the spot, feeling a sense of suspended animation, he asked, "What are you doing here?"

"Paying a visit. Is that all right?"

"I suppose," he said not quite sure. Instead of getting close, he sat on the bed. "You're looking well."

She uncrossed her legs. "Thought you hadn't noticed."

His heart revved up. He began to feel achey.

"Is Teddy Bear happy to see me?"

"I," was all he could manage.

She stood up. His T-shirt fell to her upper thighs. She walked toward him. "Can I sit on your lap?"

He nodded.

She reached for his neck, then spreading her legs, straddled him. His arms closed in on her lower back. She whispered in his ear, "Missed you, Teddy." Her warm, sweet breath turned him inside out.

She unbuckled his belt. "Now, I don't want you to strain yourself. Let me take care of you."

Ted wanted to stop her. Say, listen you just can't come in here and expect me to act like nothing's happened. But, well, there was no need to hold a grudge.

At 9 a.m. Ted awoke. Stacy was lying on her back with her head slightly turned and her mouth wide open. A little spit drained out. He let his eyes fall over her body. She was naked and spread out, as usual, leaving him on the edge of the bed. He wanted to reach over and touch her, feel the smooth, warm skin. But at what price? Waking her was never a pleasant task. She wasn't a morning person. Still, maybe things had changed. Hell, of course they'd changed. She'd coming running back. He leaned over and blew on her tit. Without waking she swatted, knocking his nose. He reared back and waited for her eyes to open. Instead, she rolled over and faced the other direction. He then decided to get up, take a shower and make some noise.

As the water pelted against his shoulders, Teddy thought hard about the situation and who had the upper hand. For once, he felt he held the cards and could make demands, have her tow the line. Not that he'd ask for much, but if she wanted to be with him there'd be certain rules, expectations – no more nights away from him, no more lame excuses for taking four hours to run out for a quart of milk. They'd have to move out of the room of course. Maybe find a rental in a mobile park, at least until he got back on his feet. He could pick up extra work as a bartender on the weekends. She'd have her days to herself and could stay with him at the bar or go back to waitressing a few hours a week to keep busy and bring in some extra cash.

The previous evening they hadn't had a chance to talk. No questions were asked, no reasons given. Just as well. Why not start fresh? He lathered up, shaved, flossed, then reached for some Old Spice aftershave. It tingled on his face. Rather than dress, he kept the towel around his waist. Maybe she'd be awake and ready for another round. But when he opened the door, she remained dead to the world, snoring like a rhino. He got dressed and headed out for her favorite breakfast, a large double cream Tim Horton coffee and an Egg McMuffin.

When he returned twenty minutes later, she was sitting at the window, smoking and wearing one of his T-shirts. Her hair was mussed as if she had just awoken. But her lips were blood red and shiny. "Hey, Teddy Bear," she said.

He walked over to the table. "I got you some breakfast." From inside his pocket he pulled out three extra creams and dropped them on the table.

She reached for the coffee. "You remembered. You're such a doll."

He leaned over and kissed her cheek. She smelled like sex. He put his hand on the T-shirt and squeezed one breast. "Teddy, you're wearing me out," she said. "I need some coffee first." He backed off and sat across from her.

"We also need to talk," she said, removing the lid from the cardboard cup.

Talk? He didn't like the sound of that. Was this another ploy for money? "Go on."

"I know what you must be wondering. Where I've been? What I've been up to? I should have let you know. You were good to me, Ted, the best. I shouldn't have taken advantage of you. I'm . . . you know, sorry."

His lips turned into a doubtful smile, as if he'd just heard a joke he didn't understand. Stacy was sorry? Hell, she'd never apologized before. Maybe she turned over a new leaf, or maybe . . . "You okay? I mean you're not sick or anything?"

"Hell, no. "

The tightness in his shoulders loosened. Thank God.

"Listen, I really appreciate you taking care of that bill I sent you. I know it must have been an inconvenience."

"Don't think about it. You're my wife. We have to look out for each other."

Her eyes shifted to the cup of coffee. Her thumb and index finger plucked at the paper lip. Something was on her mind. Ted moved the chair closer and tried reading her face. She was in another world, miles away. Taking a chance, he placed his hand on her leg above the knee. She said nothing. He felt upward along the smooth inner thigh. Her legs parted easily. How soft a woman could be. Silky. And so very warm.

Whatever preoccupation she had, seemed to have passed. Her eyes fell on him. "Teddy, I've got something to say. Well, not say, but discuss."

He reached farther, parting the moist sticky fold. Her breath caught. Suddenly, it all came back, the desperate, daytime sex they'd had in dingy, chilly motel rooms after endless hours of thruway driving and hard-ons. They had barely known each other. It had been a short two months before he sold the house and they left for Florida. So much changed in so little time. But it was worth every moment to watch her body jiggle and heave. His mouth felt dry. He stood up and unzipped his pants.

"Now, Teddy, slow down. We have to talk."

"It can wait."

Her eyes fell on him. "Pooh Bear, you're distracting me."

He stepped out of his pants. "That's the idea, isn't it?"

"You sure you can do this?"

He laughed. "Does it look like I can't? Stand up," he said, pulling her off the chair. He needed to see her naked, to imprint her body into his mind. He tugged at the shirt.

"Slow down, baby."

His body throbbed. He wanted to take her against the wall, feel hands full of ass while she hung onto him for dear life. He pulled the shirt over her head. Her breasts seemed fuller, her waist smaller. Had she lost a few pounds, been working out? Or was she just happy to see him? He swallowed hard, tweaked her tit, then ran his hands all over. Whatever the change he liked it plenty.

"Teddy – "

"Listen. Whatever you got to say can wait." The words came out gruffer than he expected. "Let's just do it." He then backed her against the wall, grabbed her legs and heaved her up.

She reached around his neck and straddled him easily.

He look down at himself and slid between her splayed-open legs. It was like cutting into soft butter. Deep inside her, he began to pump. Her hot panting breath was on his neck. She moaned with each thrust and held on tighter. He wanted to last forever, to feel her needfulness for him. He had to slow things down. He stopped and tried to relax. Looking into her watery brown eyes, he said, "Talk to me."

"You want to talk?"

Yeah, he wanted her to talk. To say how much she missed him, how he was the only one, now and forever.

She didn't respond. He had taken her breath away. "Talk to me. Tell me what you want. I can give it to you."

Her hips began move. "I . . . I . . ."

He squeezed her ass. "Tell me baby."

"Teddy, I want . . ."

He slid deep inside. "What, baby?" he said into her ear.

"Teddy . . . Teddy . . ." Her voice was breathless. "I want a divorce."

thirst

Divorce?

She pushed harder, faster.

He leaned against her, pinning her to the wall. "What did you say?"

"Now, Pooh, you told me to talk."

He felt himself getting soft. He looked at her face. "If you want a divorce, what the hell are we doing?"

"Now listen. This was your idea."

His idea? He pulled out and set her down.

"What? You may as well finish what you started."

He looked around for his pants.

"Now you're angry."

"Stacy, get dressed."

"I will not." She reached for him.

He shrugged her off. As usual he was being played for a sucker. "Leave me alone. Pack your stuff and get out."

"Fine. But I need you to sign some papers."

"I'm not signing anything."

He zipped up his pants. Some of her clothes were laying on the floor. A balled-up pair of jeans and a top. He stooped down.

Suddenly, there was a knock at the door. They exchanged glances.

"Who is it?" Ted yelled.

"Ted, it's me. Jennie."

Ted wiped his forehead. Damn.

Stacy folded her arms. "Jennie?"

He tossed Stacy her clothes. "I'm supposed to do some work at her house. Go in the bathroom and get dressed."

"Why should I?"

"Dammit. Just do it."

She stomped off and slammed the bathroom door.

Ted fumbled with a T-shirt. "Be a minute."

"Okey-dokey," came Jennie's voice.

He looked the room over. Besides wet towels, an unmade bed and fast food containers, Stacy's crap – make-up, boots, underwear – was all over the place. He'd have to reschedule in the hall. He cracked open the door and slipped out.

"Hey, Jennie." As usual she was smiling.

"Ready to go? Ted, you may need a coat." She glanced down. "And some shoes . . . Did I come too early?"

"No. It's just that something came up. An emergency you could say."

"Oh."

"Listen. I'm sorry. Maybe we could get together tomorrow night after work."

"Well, sure."

Without warning, the door behind him flew open. Jennie's expression froze. Ted turned. *Christ.* Stacy was stark naked.

"You have a girlfriend and you're giving me a hard time?"

"Stacy, get back in the room."

Jennie stepped backward. "Ted, we'll talk tomorrow."

"Like hell." Stacy reached across Ted and grabbed Jennie's arm. "Not before we have a little *tête-à-tête*."

Ted broke Stacy's hold. "Lay off."

Stacy glared at Ted. "Fine. We don't have to talk here. I'll just follow her outside. Would that be better, Ted?" Stacy stepped past him. "Come on, girlfriend," she said to Jennie.

Jennie shook her head. "But I'm not his girlfriend."

Somewhere from downstairs a door opened. "Ted," the landlady's voice floated up, "is everything okay?"

Great, all he needed was to get thrown out. Ted leaned over the banister. "Not a problem." He clamped onto Stacy's arm and spoke between clenched teeth. "I don't need a scene."

She hissed into his ear. "If you have nothing to hide, then let me talk to her."

"You want to talk to Jennie?" He pushed her into the room. "Then cover yourself up."

"Whatever."

Shell-shocked, Jennie stood motionless in the hall.

"I'm sorry about this, Jennie." He looked toward room. "But maybe it would be good to talk to Stacy. If you wouldn't mind. Just tell the truth. It would help me out."

"Sure, Ted."

Ted poked his head through the doorway. Stacy had wrapped a sheet around her shoulders and was sitting on the bed. She glared at him. Ted opened the door wider. "Come on in, Jennie."

thirst

Jennie slipped in and cowered against the wall. Ted closed the door.

"Ted's my husband." Stacy told Jennie.

Jennie nodded.

"Did he tell you he was married?"

"Well actually . . . " Jennie glanced at Ted.

Stacy pounced. "Why are you looking at him? What are you two hiding?"

Jennie raised her hands. "No. No. Ted never said anything one way or another. But there was talk around the store that he was."

"Hell, yes. He's married to me."

"Let's cut to the chase," Ted said. "Jennie, are we dating?"

"You and me? No. You offered to fix my bathtub."

"Ah-ha." Stacy faced Ted. "She may not be your girlfriend now, but what you got planned?"

Ted shook his head. "Listen Stacy. Jennie and I work together. We're friends. That's it. Why do you care anyway? You want a damn divorce."

"Yes, Ted, I do want a divorce but don't make it sound like you don't. Clearly you're moving on."

Ted shook his head. "Stacy, I'm not signing anything."

"Listen Ted. I've come all this way. We had a good thing going but it's over."

Ted stood firm. "You come in here and act like everything's fine. Then throw this at me. Tell me why."

thirst

"Why?" Stacy glared. "Don't lay a guilt trip on me."

"Guilt trip?"

Jennie chirped. "I should leave."

"Wait," said Ted. "I'm going to go with you, just like I promised. Stacy, you need to calm down. We'll talk when I get back."

"No way I'm hanging around this dump. You sign these papers Ted Blaine."

She let the sheet fall from her shoulders and jumped from the bed.

"Stacy, cover up."

"Eff-you," she yelled back.

She was bent over now, digging through some luggage. Clothes flew. "Where are those damn papers?" she said to herself.

Ted ripped the sheet from the bed and threw it over her like a tarp. She whipped around and lunged for him. "You sonofabitch."

Ted grabbed her wrists.

"Let go of me," she screamed.

In the distance, through his pulsing anger, he heard Jennie's voice. "Ted, someone's at the door."

He froze.

Sure enough, there was a faint knock. The landlady no doubt.

"Stacy, please be quiet."

"Not until you promise."

"Promise what?"

"To sign the papers."

"Okay, okay," he whispered.

Stacy stepped aside. "Well, all right then. I'll stay quiet as a mouse. I'll give you five minutes."

Ted shook his head, then cracked open the door.

"Hello, Ted."

His heart skipped a beat. *Meg?*

"I can't stay mad, Ted."

His body seized up, his jaw tightened. "This isn't a good time."

Meg's head bobbed side to side, trying to look beyond him.

"Don't be silly," she said, and pushed the door against him, throwing him off balance.

The first person Meg seemed to notice was Jennie, standing by the wall. Meg smiled. "Oh, you have company."

Ted jumped in front of his sister, trying to block any further view. "Yes. Listen, I'll call you later. We'll go out to dinner."

"Dinner? Well, sure, but – "

Ted's maneuvering wasn't enough.

"What the – "

"Hello, Meg," said Stacy.

His sister's face transformed, got hard and pale like set concrete.

Stacy looked Meg up and down. "What? Never seen a naked woman before? No, I suppose not."

"Ted, what's going on here?" Meg said.

Stacy grinned. "We're having a threesome. Wanna join us?"

Ted shook his head. "Stacy, shut up."

Crimson, Jennie said, "I'm not involved with any of this. I just work with Ted. He offered to do some work at my house. I came to pick him up."

Meg turned to Ted. "Ted, how can you expect this poor girl to stand here and be a witness to this . . . nakedness. My Lord."

"You're right, Meg." Ted said to his sister. "Go home, and I'll go with Jennie to her house. Stacy will stay here."

Stacy gave Ted a little cat smile. "Aren't you forgetting something?"

Divorce papers! Now wouldn't be the time or place. Not with Meg hovering, not with her grand plans of living together. He corralled both Jennie and Meg toward the door. "I'll meet you two downstairs. I need a couple of minutes with Stacy."

Suddenly, Meg became immovable. She turned toward Stacy. "I know why you're here."

Stacy stepped back.

Meg looked at her brother. "She wants a divorce, doesn't she?"

Ted's glance ran between the two women. How did Meg know?

"Ha! I knew it." Meg pointed her finger. "Conniving little bitch."

Stacy reached for a towel. "I don't have to listen to this."

Meg laughed. "A little late for covering up, isn't it?"

"Ted, get your loser sister out of here."

"Meg, how do you know Stacy wants a divorce?"

Meg glared at Stacy. "You tell him."

Stacy folded her arms.

"Coward." Meg turned to Ted. "You know why she's naked? Never wears clothes. She's a stripper. Venus Luv. Making a small fortune. Found her on the net. She's got a website."

"What?"

"Tracked her down."

"Why?"

"Ted, if you weren't going to get a divorce, maybe she would. Now don't get mad, but I emailed her."

"You what?"

"I told her you were sick and needed a lot of treatments, expensive treatments, that she'd have to pay for. A wifely duty."

Ted dropped to the bed. "Stacy, is that why you . . . me?"

Stacy shrugged. "I'm an angel of mercy."

Ted snorted. Pity sex. What a joke, not Stacy, but him. "Anyone got a pen?"

Ten minutes later, Meg and Stacy were gone. Jennie was waiting in the car.

Ted slipped into the front seat. "Sorry you had to see that."

Jennie smiled. "Ted, I would have crawled over hot coals to get that darn drain fixed."

125

Ted laughed. Jennie was still liquid sunshine. Clipping on the seatbelt, he then thought of his sister. He'd get the chewy cookies next time.

~~~~~

Author's Note:

The kernel for Ted Blaine's story began with an image – a young woman, an older man, in a car traveling south. But what turns an image into a story? "Teddy Bear" could have started in many spots but it was only when I focused on Ted's overriding emotion that the narrative began to take form. Suddenly, I knew what the story was about, where it would begin, and how it would end. And what was that powerful emotion? The poor man was lovesick.

~ D i s c u s s i o n   Q u e s t i o n s ~

1. Writers, like most people, have a propensity toward certain subjects, those topics that rattle around in their heads, that are never put to sleep. What recurrent themes are dominant in this collection? And of those stories that have similar themes, what makes them different?

~~~~~

2. Violence toward women is portrayed in "DMV" and "Jack." In each narrative, there is no resolution for the victim. By leaving the story unresolved, how does this affect the interpretation or impression of the piece? What are the advantages/disadvantages of ending a story on a low, conjectural note?

~~~~~

3. A story can be about a character, an event, a feeling. Also integral is conflict, a cornerstone of the human condition. Which

narrative resonated the most with you and why? Was conflict an important aspect or did you enjoy the story for a different reason?

~~~~~

4. Included in this volume are author notes at the end of each story. The author appended these comments after enjoying the afterwords of other writers. Do the notes detract or enrich the collection?

~~~~~

~ B o o k s & R e v i e w s ~

Rented Rooms, a collection of previously published short fiction, is an ensemble work of mystery, misguided love and characters who cross the line. Editorial comments for stories in *Rented Rooms*: "stands out for its physical description and dialogue" ***Pif*** . . . "very engaging, as is the tone" ***Hand Held Crime*** . . . "loved the comeuppance" ***Woman's World*** . . . "very nice work" ***Zoetrope, ALL STORY*** . . . "writing above standard" ***Barcelona Review***.

~~~~~

Paloma, a novel of romantic suspense, features a woman with three identities. Someone wants her dead but which identity is the killer after? Reviews for *Paloma*: "fast-paced, a recommended read" ***Online Review of Books and Current Affairs*** . . . "one of the best crafted books I've read in a while, a keeper" ***Literary Lighthouse Reviews*** . . . "as much about the relationship between two people as it is about the plot to kill one of them" *Rambles* . . . "really rather clever narrative" *Tregolwyn Book Reviews.*

~~~~~

thirst

Coming in 2007 . . .

Composition,
a fiction writer's guide
for the 21st century

Excerpt:

I'm standing before you, a decidedly middle-aged woman, round, doughy and blinking through smudged glasses. It's 6:00 p.m. We are in VFW post drinking bitter coffee from Styrofoam cups. I look worried and I am. It's my turn to disclose. All eyes, expectant, are on me. I clear my throat, swallow and say, "My name is Linda . . ." I pause, unsure if I should proceed. What will you think? That I'm a fool, a loser? I want to run, but I've come this far. Instead, I steady myself and say, "and I'm self published."

My confession is greeted with a pall of silence. I recoil waiting for the jeers, the scoffs and the room to empty out. Remarkably however, from the last row of seats, a voice calls out (maybe it's yours), "Good evening, Linda."

Relief sweeps through me. I am among friends . . . or at least one.

~~~~~

To learn more, please visit www.lindalavid.com

Printed in the United States
53871LVS00002B/103-204